ALSO BY

ERIC-EMMANUEL SCHMITT

The Most Beautiful Book in the World
The Woman with the Bouquet
Concerto to the Memory of an Angel
Three Women in a Mirror

INVISIBLE LOVE

Eric-Emmanuel Schmitt

INVISIBLE LOVE

*Translated from the French
by Howard Curtis*

Europa
editions

Europa Editions
214 West 29th Street
New York, N.Y. 10001
www.europaeditions.com
info@europaeditions.com

Translation by Howard Curtis
Original title: *Les deux messieurs de Bruxelles*
Translation copyright © 2014 by Europa Editions

Library of Congress Cataloging in Publication Data is available
ISBN 978-1-60945-203-2

Schmitt, Eric-Emmanuel
Invisible Love

Book design by Emanuele Ragnisco
www.mekkanografici.com

Cover image: René Magritte (1898-1967), *La reconnaissance infinie*, 1963
© 2013. BI, ADAGP, Paris/Scala, Firenze

Prepress by Grafica Punto Print – Rome

Printed in the USA

CONTENTS

TWO GENTLEMEN FROM BRUSSELS

The day a thirty-year-old man in a blue suit rang at her door and asked her if she was the Geneviève Grenier, maiden name Piastre, who had married Édouard Grenier fifty-five years earlier, on the afternoon of April 13, in Sainte-Gudule Cathedral, her first impulse was to retort that she wasn't going to take part in any TV game show and slam the door in his face. But, as usual, she was reluctant to hurt anyone's feelings, and so she suppressed the thoughts that had crossed her mind and simply said, "Yes."

Delighted with the answer, the man in the blue suit told her that his name was Demeulemeester, that he was a lawyer, and that he was here to inform her that she was the sole legal heir of Monsieur Jean Daemens.

"What?" she replied, her eyes wide with surprise.

The lawyer feared he might have committed a blunder. "Didn't you know that he was dead?"

It was worse than that: she didn't even know he had ever existed! Jean Daemens? The name rang no bells. Was her mind as impaired as her legs? Was nothing working anymore? Jean Daemens? Jean Daemens? In some vague way, she felt guilty.

"My . . . my memory isn't what it was. Tell me more. How old was this man?"

"You were born in the same year."

"What else?"

"Monsieur Daemens lived here in Brussels, at 22 Avenue Lepoutre."

"I never knew anyone in that neighborhood."

"He had a jewelry store in the Galerie de la Reine for a long time. *L'Atout coeur*, it was called."

"Oh yes, I remember that shop. Very stylish."

"He closed it down five years ago."

"I often looked in the window, but I never went in."

"Why not?"

"It was far too expensive for me . . . No, I don't know the man."

The lawyer scratched his head.

Geneviève Grenier thought it relevant to add, "Sorry."

At this, he looked up and said, articulating his words clearly, "Your secrets are your business, madame. I'm not here to pass comment on your relationship with Monsieur Daemens but to carry out his final wishes. As I've said, he made you his sole heir."

Stung by the insinuations in the lawyer's statement, Geneviève was about to defend herself when he went on, "My one question, Madame Grenier, is this: do you wish to claim the inheritance or not? Take a few days to think it over. Don't forget that, if you do claim it, you may inherit debts as well as assets."

"What?"

"According to law, once a legatee accepts the terms of a will, he is authorized to receive the assets but is also obliged to settle the debts if there are any."

"And are there any?"

"There are sometimes."

"But in this case?"

"The law forbids me from answering that question, madame."

"You must know! Tell me!"

"It's the law, madame! I took an oath."

"My dear monsieur, I'm old enough to be your mother. You wouldn't lure your poor old mother into a trap, would you?"

"I can't tell you, madame. Here's my card. Come to my office when you've made up your mind."

The man clicked his heels and took his leave.

In the days that followed, Geneviève looked at the question from every angle.

When she phoned her friend Simone to ask her for advice, she presented the case as something that was happening to a neighbor.

"Before your neighbor makes up her mind," Simone immediately said, "she needs to find out a bit more about this man. What work did he do?"

"He owned a jewelry store."

"Doesn't mean anything. He might have been rich, but the place might just as easily have gone bust."

"He closed it down five years ago."

"You see! Bankrupt!"

"Come on, Simone, at our age people don't want to go on working."

"What else?"

"He lived on Avenue Lepoutre."

"Did he own his own apartment?"

"I think so."

"Not enough. If his business was going downhill, he probably mortgaged the apartment."

"If he did, who would know?"

"His bank, but they'd never give out the information. How did he die?"

"Why?"

"Well, if your neighbor's friend died of an illness, that's a good sign. If, on the other hand, he killed himself, I'd be worried. It'd mean he was up to his neck in debt."

"Not necessarily, Simone. He might have killed himself because he'd had bad news. That he had cancer for example."

"Mmm . . . "

"Or that his children had died in a plane crash."

"Did he have children?"

"No. They aren't mentioned in his will."

"Mmm . . . You're not going to convince me a suicide isn't suspicious!"

"My neighbor never said anything about suicide."

"Come to think of it, your neighbor might have bumped him off! He's her lover, she finds out he's put her in his will, so she kills him."

"Simone, we don't even know how he died!"

"That shows how clever she is."

"He wasn't her lover!"

"Oh, Geneviève, don't be so naive! He leaves her his entire fortune, and she wasn't his mistress? I find that hard to swallow!"

The question of whether to accept or decline always led to others: Who was this man? What connection was there between them? So, after getting a second negative opinion from a cousin in the insurance business, Geneviève decided to give up asking for advice.

From morning to evening, she leaned first in one direction and then in the other. Accept or decline? It was a big gamble! Even though she was losing sleep, she was rather enjoying this mental agitation: at last something adventurous was happening in her life . . . She couldn't stop weighing the pros and cons.

After seventy-two hours, she made up her mind.

The woman who appeared at the office of the lawyer Demeulemeester had decided to be a gambler. Since the cautious thing to do would be to refuse the offer, she was going to accept it! She hated moderation, having spent too much of her life being moderate and restrained. And anyway, at the age of eighty, she was hardly running any risks. Even if she did inherit debts, she'd never be able to pay them off, since all she had was the tiny allowance from the state that a senior citizen was expected to live on. Even if she owed several million, nobody would dream of reducing her meager pension. But she preferred not to develop this line of thought, afraid she might discover that her supposed recklessness would prove to be her cleverest move, that in taking a risk she wasn't actually taking any risks at all . . .

As it turned out, she had made the right decision! What she was inheriting was, in a word, a fortune: a lot of money in the bank, three apartments in Brussels, two of them rented out to tenants, all the furniture, paintings and works of art in storage at 22 Avenue Lepoutre, and, last but not least, a house in the south of France. As testimony to her newfound status, the lawyer offered to manage her inheritance for her.

"I'll think about it, monsieur. Wasn't there a letter with the will?"

"No."

"Any document for me?"

"No."

"What on earth possessed this man to choose me?"

"He didn't have any family."

"All right, but why me?"

The lawyer stared at her in silence. He was starting to have his doubts. Either, as he had supposed, she had been the man's mistress and preferred to be discreet about it, or she was telling the truth, and he was dealing with the strangest case he had ever come across . . .

"You must have known him well," Geneviève insisted.

"No, my predecessor dealt with him. He was already on our files when I took over this practice."

"Where is he buried?"

Realizing that, if he wanted to keep Geneviève as his client, he had to show that he was willing to please, the lawyer disappeared, gave some orders to his clerks, and returned five minutes later, carrying a square sheet of paper.

"Ixelles Cemetery, Avenue 1, Block 2, fifth plot on the left."
Geneviève made her way there that very day.

*

The weather was foul. A murky light poured down from the
overcast sky, emphasizing the grayness of the concrete walls
and making the faces of the pedestrians look sullen. Even
though it wasn't raining, the streets were wet, a threat more
than a memory . . .

The bus dropped Geneviève in front of the three cafés that
framed the entrance to the cemetery. Behind the windows,
nobody was sitting at the tables, and the waiters were yawning
glumly. No funerals today . . . Drawing her scarf more tightly
around her neck, Geneviève shivered at the thought of those
waiters' tasks: making comments on death, serving herb tea to
widows and lemonades to orphans, pouring beer for men
thirsty for forgetfulness. The table napkins were probably used
more for brushing away tears than wiping mouths . . .

Since the monumental wrought iron gate would not deign
to open for her, Geneviève went in through the small gate on
the left, nodded to the municipal employee in his green uniform, and came to a circular space surrounded by oaks. The
gravel crunched as she turned onto the avenue. "Leave,
stranger," it seemed to cry, "go back where you came from."
Yes, they were right, she had no place in this city of the rich.
Even though the houses of this city were vaults or mau-
soleums, their luxury, their pretentious statuary, their solemn
obelisks reminded her that, being an insignificant, penniless
woman, she had never known any of the residents. Some of
the family monuments along the row of blue cedars were two
hundred years old. Geneviève wondered why only the rich
made so much of their family trees. Didn't the poor have
ancestors?

Keeping her head down, she kept walking, telling herself that she could never afford a plot here.

Except that now she could . . .

Horrified by these calculations, she shivered and made the sign of the cross to protect herself both from the place and from her wandering mind.

"1 . . . 2 . . . 3 . . . 4 . . . 5. Here it is!"

The grave, its dark granite so polished that the leaning trees were reflected in it, bore the name Jean Daemens in gold lettering. To the right of the name, a photograph set into the gravestone showed its owner at the age of forty, dark-haired and dark-eyed, with open, clear-cut, virile features and full lips, smiling happily.

"What a handsome man!"

She didn't know him. She had never had any dealings with him. Definitely not. And yet there was something familiar about his face . . . But what? It must be something to do with his physical type . . . So many dark-haired males had those Mediterranean features, you think you've met them before. Maybe she'd come across him without noticing him . . . Once, maybe even twice . . . Where? In any case, she had never spoken to him: she was sure of that!

She continued gazing at the photograph. Why had he chosen her? What lay behind his generosity?

Could it be that she had a brother she never knew about, a twin brother? . . . No, that was absurd! Her parents would have told her! And he would surely have made his presence known to his own sister sooner or later, wouldn't he?

That brought up a new question: why hadn't this Jean Daemens put in an appearance while he was alive? Why had he shown signs of life only after he was dead?

The mystery man was still smiling from the dark gray stone.

Geneviève had the embarrassing impression that her benefactor was staring at her out of his photograph. "Th-thank

you," she stammered. "Thank you for your gift—it was wonderful, and so unexpected. Only, you'll have to explain some-
time, won't you?"

The light hit the portrait. She took that as a promise.

"Good. I . . . I'm counting on you."

Suddenly she burst into nervous laughter. How could she
be so foolish as to talk out loud to a gravestone?

Turning her head, she discovered next to it—in plot number 4—a similar grave to Jean Daemens's. More than similar—
exactly the same! Apart from the name and the photograph,
everything—the size of the stone, its color, the thin brass
cross—was the same as its neighbor: the same gold lettering,
the same typography, the same overall design.

"'Laurent Delphin,'" she read. "Oh, look, this one died five
years earlier."

This similarity suggested a connection between the two
graves, or rather between the two men. Geneviève examined
the photograph. It showed a handsome, fair-haired man of
about thirty, whom she found just as attractive as Jean
Daemens. No, it was time to put a stop to this speculation.

"I'm going crazy . . ."

She turned back to Jean Daemens with an apologetic
expression on her face, made a slight bow, and noticed that,
unlike the other graves, his had no flowers. Had he foreseen
that nobody would ever lay flowers on his grave? Vowing to
come back soon and leave a bouquet, she set off back to the
gate.

"All the same," she said to herself as she turned off the
avenue, "what a magnificent looking man!" Whereas that
morning she had considered herself lucky to even receive such
a gift, she now felt flattered that her benefactor was so handsome.

Which meant that the mystery of his intentions was becoming more unbearable to her with every passing second.

"Why? Why him and why me?"

* * *

Fifty-five years earlier, the bells of Sainte-Gudule Cathedral pealed out. In front of the altar, the young and beautiful Geneviève Piastre, fine as a lily in her white tulle dress, was marrying a strapping lad named Édouard Grenier, familiarly known as Eddy, who was blushing in embarrassment in his hired suit—in his job as a mechanic, he was more used to overalls. The two of them looked radiant, full of enthusiasm, impatient to be happy. It was thanks to an uncle that they had been able to have their wedding in this prestigious cathedral, where even the royal family held their celebrations, rather than in their gloomy neighborhood church. The priest cosseted them like two precious pieces of confectionery while, behind them, family and friends looked forward eagerly to celebrating until late into the night. It was obvious that Geneviève was entering on the happiest days of her life . . .

It would never have occurred to her to look beyond the rows of seats occupied by her guests and see what was happening at the other end of the vast cathedral, close to the main door through which she had entered, heart pounding, on her father's arm.

In the shadow of the penultimate column, protected by the statue of Simon the Zealot holding a golden saw, two men were kneeling in meditation, their demeanor not so unlike that of the couple occupying the limelight up there at the altar.

When the priest asked Eddy Grenier if he would take Geneviève as his lawful wedded wife, one of the two men, the brown-haired one, uttered a firm yes. Then, when the priest asked Geneviève the corresponding question, the fair-haired

man blushed and also consented. In spite of the distance separating them from the ceremony, they were acting as if the min-
ister of God, there in the yellow light of the stained-glass windows, were addressing them.

"I now pronounce you man and wife," the priest said, and
as the official bride and groom kissed each other on the lips,
with the figure of Christ looking down on them benevolently,
the unofficial spouses did the same in their corner. Just as
Eddy and Geneviève exchanged rings to the sound of a hymn
played by the organ, the brown-haired man took a case from
his pocket, extracted two rings, and discreetly slipped them on
his and the other man's fingers.

Nobody had noticed them.

And nobody paid any attention to them when, once the
service was over, they remained on their knees, praying, while
the wedding party dispersed down the central nave.

During the ritual congratulations in front of the cathedral,
the two men continued to meditate in the charitable half-light.
When the cheering and the car horns had subsided outside and
they at last made up their minds to move, they came out onto
the top of the empty steps, with no photographer to record the
moment, with no family members to celebrate their happiness
by throwing rice and applauding, and with no witness other
than the Gothic tower of the town hall, at the top of which the
archangel Michael was slaying a dragon in the dazzling sunlight.

They rushed to the brown-haired man's apartment at 22
Avenue Lepoutre and closed the shutters. They were freer than
Geneviève and Eddy: they didn't need to wait until nightfall to
express their love for each other beneath the sheets.

*

Much to his own astonishment, Jean had fallen in love with
Laurent.

Since he had reached adulthood, Jean had amassed a great many fleeting encounters, and had had many lovers for whom he had felt nothing. His sensual appetites had turned him into a hunter, and he had spent hours cruising bars and saunas and parks and smoky nightclubs—he hated cigarette smoke—his head battered by music he also hated, in search of prey to take home with him.

He had thought he liked this carefree, dissolute existence until he met Laurent, but from their first kisses, he realized that it was neither as wonderful nor as audacious as he had thought. It might have provided him with pleasures, orgasms, narcissistic ecstasies, but it had also bred a kind of cynicism in him. His lack of commitment had turned him into a Don Juan, doomed to endlessly start over again. He had reduced other men to the satisfaction their bodies gave him. The more he had assuaged his sexual urges, the less he had appreciated the company of men. He had fucked so many of them that he had stopped respecting them.

Laurent had restored his taste, his esteem for life. This fair-haired young man, an electrician at the Théâtre Royal du Parc, put as much enthusiasm into talking or shopping or cooking as into making love. Everything excited him. His arrival had started a revolution in Jean, helping him to discover love where previously he had known only physical pleasure. Being of a vigorous temperament, Jean reacted to this upheaval by going to extremes: he praised Laurent to the skies, showered him with gifts, smothered him with kisses, and threw himself on him with a desire that was insatiable.

That was why Jean had been so determined to consecrate their relationship. Since society did not allow the legal union of two men, he had come up with a subterfuge. It was not that Jean and Laurent found being in a sexual minority any kind of burden. They were both too glad just to be alive for that. They even derived a kind of pride from their situation as outsiders, the pride of those who, knowing they are rare, feel the thrill of the initiated: they were part of both the visible world and an invisible world, ordinary society and a clandestine society. Day by day, they hardly cared that what was granted to the masses was denied them! But if they really wanted it, they would have to get it by trickery . . .

And so it was that they married simultaneously with Eddy and Geneviève, in Sainte-Gudule Cathedral, on the afternoon of April 13.

It was pure chance that had led the two couples to share the service, and their connection would have stopped there if Laurent had not made the romantic gesture of tearing the wedding announcement from the town hall notice board. A few days later, he stuck this paper in their scrapbook, and then made a copy of it, this time celebrating the union of Jean Daemens and Laurent Delphin, a fake they both regarded as completely genuine.

Thanks to its presence in their scrapbook, the surname Grenier became familiar to them. Consequently, when the newspaper *Le Soir* announced the birth of Johnny Grenier, the son of Eddy and Geneviève, they lingered over the paragraph, deeply moved. That morning, they felt—perhaps for the first time—a purely homosexual feeling, the painful realization that their love, however strong it was, would never bear fruit.

They attended the christening.

This time, the uncle who had previously landed Sainte-Gudule Cathedral had been unable to find Geneviève and Eddy a more elegant venue than their parish church, Notre-Dame-Immaculée, where a wheezy harmonium stood in for an organ and the priest's spluttered sermon oozed from ancient gray loudspeakers that looked like lampshades. This did not bother Geneviève, engrossed as she was in the joy of motherhood, or Jean and Laurent, who were overwhelmed by this birth. Only Eddy was upset. There in the middle of the yellowish church with its grimy pews, its rudimentary stained-glass windows, its dark statues of polished wood more over-loaded with plastic flowers than a concierge's lodge, the mechanic had come down to earth: he was twenty-six, and he was bored by marriage. Yes, Geneviève was as lively and pas-sionate as ever, and still in love with him, but married life made him feel guilty about everything: meeting his pals in a bar, drinking too much, talking too much, casually flirting with girls, wolfing down junk—cones of French fries or bags of licorice—rather than the dishes lovingly prepared by Geneviève, lying late in bed with his hands behind his head and the radio blaring away, lounging about the apartment in his shorts, in other words, behaving as he had before. He hated having to watch his step, forcing himself to improve, to become clean and reasonable and responsible and faithful. It was against nature! Did he have to endure all that just so that he could have sex with his wife as often as he liked? It seemed a high price to pay . . . Worse still, when he saw that red-faced brat Johnny screaming in his swaddling clothes, he foresaw that things weren't going to get any better.

Although he was making an effort to put on a good show during the ceremony, his moroseness did not pass unnoticed by the two men sitting at the back of the church. Jean and Laurent were shocked. Didn't the stupid lump realize how lucky he was to be starting a family? What an oaf! They shifted all their sympathy to Geneviève, who was radiant.

The next day, they had a baby carriage delivered, with a note, supposedly from the local social services, congratulating the new parents.

*

Life resumed for the two couples. Each was moving at its own pace toward its own essential truth.

Jean and Laurent felt no diminution of their happiness. After conceiving a number of artistic projects that would allow him to work with Laurent in the theater, Jean had resigned himself to the fact that he had no talent. Feeling no bitterness, he had bought a shop with his father's money and had started selling jewelry. Since he had good taste and women liked him for his good manners and excellent advice, the business soon prospered. *L'Atout coeur* became the place to go for the fashionable ladies of Brussels.

Jean and Laurent were in the full flower of their love. They did nothing to hide the fact that they lived together, but nor did they flaunt it. They felt no shame, but nor did they protest. Live and let live, summed up their position. Nevertheless, influenced by libertarian ideals, society was becoming more tolerant, and the government responded to militant pressure by outlawing discrimination against those who loved their own sex. Although Jean and Laurent appreciated this relaxing of attitudes, their own viewpoint hadn't changed. Existing on the sidelines, out of sight of prying eyes, contributed to their happiness. They were still those illicit spouses who had married in the shadows, concealed behind a pillar in the cathedral.

Made all the sharper by this lack of outward show, their physical passion for each other was as strong as ever.

Eddy and Geneviève were launched on quite a different path. Johnny's screaming and whining and illnesses had provided Eddy with an excuse to grow more distant. After his day's work at the garage, he would spend hours with his buddies, drinking or playing cards, and only come home to sleep. Geneviève had noticed this, but instead of complaining she blamed herself: the reason Eddy was turning away from her was because she was too exhausted to take care of herself, because she was breastfeeding, because the only things she ever talked about were diapers, washing, and baby food.

A daughter was born.

Eddy suggested calling her Minnie, like Mickey Mouse's girlfriend! Excited by the idea, he loved to whisper this name to her every time he lifted her in his arms and would laugh until he was breathless. Horrified as she was, Geneviève, fearing that Eddy's fragile love for his children might turn to hate if she objected, accepted the name in the hope that it would help Minnie to capture her father's affection.

Jean and Laurent were traveling abroad at the time and were unaware that there had been a second baby. Although Geneviève was disappointed not to receive a gift from social services as she had the previous time, she consoled herself by using the sophisticated baby carriage she already owned.

*

Ten years passed.

Jean and Laurent thought about Eddy and Geneviève from time to time, but vaguely, with a kind of languid nostalgia. Those faces were part of their youth, and their youth was slowly receding. They made no attempt to find out anything about that other couple that existed only within the gilded frame of their happy memories.

Once again it was chance that moved things along.

Jean had hired a cleaning woman for his shop, an Italian named Angela, a big, honest, forthright woman who lived in the working class neighborhood of the Marolles. Angela was a real chatterbox. When, feather duster in hand, she mentioned during one of her daily monologues that her neighbors were called Grenier—which she pronounced with four "r"s instead of two—Jean gave a start.

Claiming an interest in her stories, he shrewdly questioned her.

What he found out upset him.

Eddy Grenier had been fired from the garage where he had

worked—his boss had finally tired of his laziness and poor timekeeping—and Geneviève had had to find a job. Being good with her hands, she had established herself as a dressmaker, working from home, which allowed her to keep an eye on her children. Not that Eddy was grateful in any way. Complaining endlessly, he would grab a few banknotes from her then leave to roam the streets.

That evening, claiming that he had a delivery to make, Jean offered to give Angela a lift home.

When they got to Rue Haute, he saw a man in a polo shirt swaggering along the sidewalk and stroking the buttocks of the redhead by his side.

"*Che miseria!*" Angela muttered. "*Ecco il mio vicino.*"

Jean found it hard to connect this strutting figure with the image of the slim, nervous, awkward bridegroom in front of the altar in the cathedral, an image that had remained engraved in his brain. Eddy had filled out a lot, his features had grown broader, he shifted more air when he moved. His gestures, his facial expressions—everything about him exuded vulgarity. His weight seemed the expression of his true nature, which had been dormant in his youth: his extra pounds were a physical symbol of his moral collapse.

Jean closed his eyes.

"Is something wrong, Monsieur Daemens?"

"No. I was just feeling sorry for that man's wife."

"Poor thing. He cheats on her *senza vergogna.*"

By the time Jean dropped Angela outside her squat building on Rue des Renards, he had learned that the neighborhood had disowned Eddy but thought highly of Geneviève. In a way, she had been ennobled by her resigned attitude, and her dignified sadness earned her the compassion of the customers who brought her their clothes to mend.

That night, in the kitchen of their apartment on Avenue Lepoutre, Jean reported these events to Laurent.

"He has girlfriends and doesn't even hide it?" Laurent said with a frown. "What a pig! You should always be discreet, shouldn't you?"

"Always."

The two lovers looked deep into each other's eyes, each understanding the other's meaning. Then they resumed their activities, one peeling the vegetables, the other laying the table. Through this exchange, they had confirmed their pact.

Jean and Laurent had no illusions. They knew how hard it is for a man to resist temptation, but they also knew what women often refuse to believe: that yielding to an impulse has no consequences. A male won't love his partner any less if he has slept with someone else. Heart and body are unconnected. Where a man commits his penis, he does not necessarily commit his feelings.

There was a tacit agreement between Jean and Laurent: they were faithful in spirit, however unfaithful in the flesh. The forbidden thing was to flaunt it or to become infatuated. To the extent that any flings went unnoticed and never led to anything, they were tolerated. As neither of them did anything to castrate the other, Jean and Laurent still loved each other.

That was why they reproached Eddy for his boorishness and despised him for humiliating his wife—having a bit on the side didn't need to be advertised and didn't have to cause any suffering.

In the months that followed, they thought a great deal about this other couple whose decline bothered them so much. They would have liked to intervene, to slow the process of decay, but what could they do? And what right did they have anyway?

Whenever they talked about it, they realized the extent of the gulf that existed between them and the other couple. They might have lamented the fact that they had no children, but at least they weren't living together just for the sake of the children! They might be a male couple, but this abnormality paradoxically made their lives easier, since two people of the same sex can understand each other better than two people of opposite sexes. Was there an advantage perhaps in being outsiders?

*

Christmas came, and Angela informed Jean in her morning chatter that her neighbor, Madame Grenier, had just had another baby.

"*Quale cretino*, it wasn't enough for him to chase after anything that moves, he had to try it on again with his old lady! *Povera* Geneviève! Now she has four mouths to feed, *un marito incapace* and three kids!"

Returning home, Jean announced the birth to Laurent.

Once again, they attended the christening. Hidden at the back of the church, they saw the members of the original wedding party after fifteen years, some easily identifiable even though they were more wrinkled and stooped, and others not, the babies having become teenagers and the teenagers mature adults. But the main focus of their curiosity was Eddy and Geneviève.

Geneviève had not changed much. Slim, fine-featured, she had lost just a little of her glow—probably along with her illusions . . . At the same time, the nervous way in which she held the baby betrayed something of her discomfort: she was clinging to him, as if this was her last chance to proclaim silently to the gathering, "You see, I'm still his wife! You see, Eddy still loves me!" The poor woman could not accept that her life was a disaster.

As for Eddy, he strutted about in a conceited manner, like a rooster that has demonstrated it can satisfy several females. He never so much as glanced at Geneviève, nor did he pay any attention to the older children, Johnny and Minnie. No, he only had eyes for the pretty women in the congregation, and took baby Claudia in his arms simply to offer them the image of a caring male, knowing this was an image that gave them all a thrill.

Jean and Laurent were dismayed by what they saw. It was clear to them that this couple was continuing its descent into hell. The only question was: When would they touch rock bottom?

Returning home, Jean and Laurent made love with unusual ardor, eager to be reassured, as if entwined arms or legs were a refuge from the violence of the world.

*

Two years flew by.

At the shop, listening to Angela's chatter, Jean would, from time to time, glean a few details about the Greniers, who continued to self-destruct while remaining together.

Then one day Angela informed him that Geneviève was pregnant again, even though she was pushing forty.

"*Non capisco niente!* When you live with a brute like that, you take the pill, don't you, Monsieur Daemens?"

"Well . . . "

"I'm sorry! I'm talking to you about a world you don't know. You're a gentleman, *non farebbe mai soffrire una signora.*"

Because Jean was so virile and so tender and charming to women, they rarely suspected that he might not desire them. Angela assumed that he had clandestine affairs with some of his distinguished customers. As for his friend Laurent, from the moment she had met him, she had supposed he led the same kind of life. As an Italian woman, she was used to men spending a lot of time together, and had never suspected a thing.

"The worst of it, Monsieur Daemens, is that Geneviève seems to be happy to be carrying this child! Oh, yes! *Esibisce* her big belly like a queen at the window of her coach. *A quarant'anni!*"

This time, there was no ad in *Le Soir*: the well-to-do uncle who always paid for the ads and who had once arranged it so that they could marry in Sainte-Gudule Cathedral had just passed away.

Nevertheless, informed by Angela as to which church the ceremony was being held in, Jean and Laurent attended the christening of the new baby, David.

The daily flea market on Place du Jeu-de-Balle was just coming to an end, leaving the area in front of the church looking like a garbage dump. Scraps of newspaper, foam from torn armchairs, broken coat hangers, crushed cartons, and chipped bowls lay on the wet paving stones. As the last vendors loaded their remaining stock onto graffiti-covered vans, two black women stuffed the garbage that interested them into plastic bags while an old man in a pea jacket and fishermen's boots, pretending to be there by chance, was also sifting through leftovers.

Pausing outside the red brick church, Jean and Laurent wondered what they were doing here. It was routine that had brought them. They hadn't really wanted to come. The game had stopped being fun. Having blamed Eddy for years, they now trained their criticism on Geneviève. Why didn't she react? Why, instead of throwing the son of a bitch out, was she still giving herself to him? Either she was pathologically weak, or she still loved him, which made her just as much of a pathological case. Not knowing which was the correct answer—cowardice or masochism—they decided to flee that hellish relationship. What connection did they have with it any longer? None at all. On the threshold of the church, they vowed that this was the last time they would take any interest in Eddy and Geneviève, and that was final!

They went inside Notre-Dame-Immaculée, known as the Spanish church because it was attended by so many Spanish-speaking immigrants, a curious building that looked more like a dining hall with its yellow walls and ceiling lights than a place of worship. They stepped over bouquets of artificial flowers to get to their place and observed the activity around the dark wooden altar.

Geneviève was transformed. She looked ten years younger and eight inches taller. A vision of loveliness, elegant even though simply dressed, she clasped the child to her, making no attempt to hide her emotion. A sullen, unshaven Eddy trailed after her like a dog on a leash and stared at the guests in a hostile manner. He had lost all the swagger he had shown at previous christenings.

When the door creaked behind them and a shadowy figure slipped into the church on the right-hand side, opposite from where they were, Jean and Laurent had their first inkling of what was going on. The dark-haired, Spanish-looking man sunk into a pew, clearly terrified of being seen.

The service began.

A vague smile on her lips, Geneviève would glance from time to time at the far corners, sometimes to the right, sometimes to the left, which suggested that she sensed a presence but couldn't actually see anything. For a brief moment, she lifted up baby David and displayed him to the horizon.

The Spaniard followed the service in every detail, dutifully kneeling or standing, mumbling the prayers, humming the hymns and punctuating the ceremony with judiciously placed amens.

Jean and Laurent winked at each other: the man was behaving just as they had done during the wedding in Sainte-Gudule. There was no doubt that he regarded this celebration as his.

"That's the father," Laurent whispered.

"Not bad."

"Not bad at all," said Laurent. "He looks like you."

Jean was so flattered, he could think of nothing to say in reply.

"In addition," Laurent went on, "if my eyes aren't deceiving me, that baby there is definitely going to be dark."

"Hmm . . . Anyway, I'm delighted to learn that Geneviève has taken a lover. I like her more than ever."

"Me too," replied Laurent. "Especially as she has the same tastes as me."

Jean felt a lump in his throat. After fifteen years of living together, a compliment like that moved him even more than it had in the early days of their relationship.

Laurent turned his attention to the sullen-looking Eddy. "The husband probably doesn't know, but he smells a rat. Look at his face. Now he knows what it feels like to be cheated on."

"Yes, at last!"

They both laughed.

Across the nave from them, the Spaniard bristled at this and shot them an angry look.

Instead of silencing them, his indignation provoked giggles in the two men, and they had to leave the church in order not to disturb the service.

Once outside, on Place du Jeu-de-Balle, they got back in the car and wiped their eyes.

"We got out in time. If Eddy Grenier had seen you up close, I'm sure he'd have assumed you were the father."

"Stop saying we look alike!"

"Come on, it's obvious . . . Look, there he is right now."

The Spaniard was just leaving the church, running out between the road menders and the hoboes, afraid of being seen before the service was over.

"He has your hair, your figure," Laurent said. "Okay, the

face is different, and probably a few other details I can't check, however much I'd like to."

"So you still love me, do you?"

"Seems like it," Laurent muttered with a shrug. "How about you?"

"Let's go home and I'll show you . . ."

Jean started the engine and drove impatiently to Avenue Lepoutre.

Every time they got back from the churches where they had been spying on the Greniers, Jean and Laurent made love. Every time, their lovemaking was fueled by a different feeling. This time, there was a kind of violence in it, a controlled violence of course, which meant "I really want you" and revived the magic of their first embrace.

*

The birth of David brought about a rebirth in their relationship. Jean and Laurent forgot the vow they had made on the threshold of the church—never to see Eddy or Geneviève again—and followed events in the Marolles with great interest.

Angela's items of gossip being somewhat fragmentary, Laurent decided to investigate for himself. He had discovered that some of his fellow electricians and stagehands at the Théâtre Royal du Parc lived in the Marolles, and so he got into the habit of going with them to the local bars, and even took up bowling.

Within a few months, he managed to find out that the Spaniard wasn't a Spaniard, he was Italian, his name was Giuseppe, and he, too, was married, which explained his secretiveness.

Although nobody was aware of the affair between Geneviève and Giuseppe, anyone seeing Geneviève cross the street with her baby carriage, full of beauty and energy and self-confidence, could sense that this woman was blossoming, physically and emotionally.

At last, Angela announced that in one of the quarrels she overheard through the wall Geneviève had asked for a divorce.

"He's refusing, of course. Without her, that good-for-nothing will be penniless. But she's giving as good as she gets, is our Geneviève. I can hardly recognize her."

"Tell me, Angela, do you think she has a lover?"

"*Scherza*! When you're lumbered with *un pezzo* like that, *sarebbe giudizioso* to take a lover, but not her! *Santa madonna* . . ."

As soon as Angela left the store, Jean turned to Laurent and said in a voice trembling with emotion, "Our little Geneviève's a fighter."

"Yes. I'm proud of her."

"Is she going to make it?"

"If you saw her with her David in her arms," Laurent cried, "you'd know she will."

Jean and Laurent discussed Geneviève, Eddy, Giuseppe, David, Minnie, Johnny, and Claudia as if they were talking about their own family. Without their realizing it, the story of that other couple had become part of their life. It was as if they were close friends.

It never even crossed their minds that if anyone had mentioned their two names—Jean Daemens and Laurent Delphin—to the Greniers, the latter would not have known who they were talking about.

Angela's next piece of gossip was that her neighbor was going to move house. Even though her husband was refusing a divorce, she was going to present him with a fait accompli and move out with her four children. Jean did his best to conceal his joy, but then took advantage of Angela going out to run an errand and called Laurent at the theater to tell him the news.

That evening, they went to L'Écailler du Roi on Place des Sablons to celebrate. There, surrounded by blue decor that resembled the sea, they drank copious amounts of champagne. What factory worker or cleaning woman living in the damp buildings of the Marolles would have imagined that above their heads, in the upper town, two men were sitting in one of the most expensive restaurants in the city and celebrating the emancipation of one of their neighbors?

They spent the following Monday trying to figure out a way to help Geneviève move out while remaining anonymous and not arousing any suspicion. They had thought up a number of plausible scenarios by the time Angela said to Jean in the shop on Tuesday, "You know what happened, *Signor* Daemens? Eddy Grenier had a stroke! Just like that!"

"Is he dead?"

"No. They rushed him to emergency. Now he's in intensive care. I hope God sends *questo diavolo* straight to hell."

"That's not very Catholic of you, Angela."

"Eddy won't be any more *caldo* in the ass down there than he is up here: he's always kept it close to the oven. *Almeno*, he'll pay for his cheating. *Sì, lo so*, it's not a very Christian thing to say, but *questo mostro* has never been very Christian either, so . . ."

Given that he shared her opinion, Jean was perfectly prepared to grant her absolution.

For a few hours, Jean and Laurent fervently hoped that Eddy would die. They did not feel bad in any way about thinking this. Their one fear was that the incident would set back Geneviève's happiness.

Angela kept Jean up to date with the situation. At first, Eddy's condition was stable. Then she reported "a slight improvement." Finally, she announced triumphantly that Eddy had been moved out of intensive care and into the regular cardiac ward. Over the days, without even realizing it, Angela had forgotten her curse on Eddy and had started seeing his illness through her neighbor's eyes, delighting in tiny improvements, desiring a speedy recovery. So carried away was she by her good heart, it would not have been a surprise if she had taken flowers to this man she detested.

A few weeks later, as she swept the floor, Angela said, "Did I ever tell you about my neighbor, Monsieur Daemens, a nice woman named Geneviève Grenier?"

Jean pricked up his ears. "The one who's supposed to be leaving her husband?" he said casually.

"*Ecco*! Only now she isn't."

"What?"

"He's coming home from hospital today. He's going to need physical therapy."

"There are institutions for that."

"That's what I said, *Signor* Daemens! *Parola per parola* it's what I told her! And you know what she replied? That he's still the father of her children, that she'd never forgive herself if she abandoned him *in questo stato*, that she's given up her other plans. I didn't quite understand what she *suggerisce* by these 'other plans' because, apart from moving, *non ha menzionato* that she was changing jobs . . . Actually, I promised I'd go help her at the hospital. That's at five o'clock! Do you mind if *tolgo* a few minutes? I'll make it up tomorrow."

"Better still, Angela, I'll drop you there, I have a delivery to make."

"*Fantastico!*"

At five o'clock, Jean drove Angela to the Saint-Pierre Hospital, waited until she had entered the lobby, then went and parked his car a short distance away and took up his position in a café on Rue Haute.

Half an hour later, Angela reappeared, carrying a couple of cardboard suitcases. Behind her came Geneviève, pushing a wheelchair in which Eddy sat slumped, pale-faced and dribbling, moving at the slightest jolt like a bag of meat. The whole of his right side was paralyzed.

Above that lifeless face, Geneviève's face seemed just as expressionless, her complexion waxy, her lips pale, her absent gaze fixed straight ahead.

Jean wanted to leap out and scream, "Leave him, he's ruined your life and he's going to keep ruining it. Go back to Giuseppe right now!"

But from the care she took in maneuvering the wheelchair, avoiding the bumps in the road, making sure that the blanket was protecting the patient from the cold, Jean realized that Geneviève would never go back on her decision. She was sacrificing her happiness, allowing herself to be walled alive in a tomb. With suicidal generosity, she had placed her pity for Eddy over her love for Giuseppe.

She passed a few yards from Jean, and, seeing her gently moving that wreck that had once been Eddy through the streets of the Marolles, his anger was replaced by admiration. What dignity! "For better or worse," the priest had said beneath the shimmering stained-glass windows of Sainte-Gudule. That was what she had committed herself to, and she was keeping her word. The "better" had been brief. The "worse" had already lasted a long time, and looked set to last much longer. Jean felt pitiful in comparison. Would he be capable of such self-denial?

Shaken, he got back in his car and for a long time drove aimlessly through the tunnels that surrounded the city, lost in thought.

When Laurent heard about Geneviève's change of mind, he was just as upset. How could you put anything before happiness? He too would never have imagined . . . Although they both disapproved of Geneviève, she was forcing them to look at things differently.

That evening, Laurent asked Jean, "Would you still love me if I became disabled?"

"I don't know. You've never brought me anything but joy. What about you?"

"The same."

They pondered this. Then Laurent said, "Basically, there's no merit in our loving each other . . ."

Jean nodded.

They looked at each other, both stirred by a mixture of emotions. Should they put each other to the test to measure the extent of their love? That was absurd. They broke off this conversation and went out to see a movie.

*

The months that followed confirmed the magnitude of Geneviève's sacrifice.

Since Laurent had gotten into the habit of joining his colleagues in the bars of the Marolles, he often saw Giuseppe, who was looking increasingly sullen and demoralized.

"According to the owner of the Perroquet," he said one day to Jean, "Giuseppe's planning to go back to Italy soon. He says the reason he's so glum is that he's homesick."

"What a mess. And what about David? Does this mean he'll never know his real father?"

"That's the fate of illegitimate children. The mother decides."

The grim turn that events had taken—chronicle of a disaster foretold—lessened their interest in the Grenier family.

Almost in spite of themselves, they turned their attention away from them, made new friends, traveled more.

They were probably afraid . . . Which of us, coming into contact with misfortune, hasn't feared infection?

Then, when we realize that misfortune can't be spread like a virus, it is no longer misfortune that we fear, but our own reaction to it. The inertia that keeps us in painful situations opens the door to the negative forces within us, the forces that lead us to the precipice and make us lean over to look down at the seething crater, to move closer to its lava, to smell its hot, fatal breath . . .

It was their instinct for life that made Jean and Laurent distance themselves from the Greniers.

*

Several years passed.

Jean and Laurent were approaching their fifties, a difficult time for men. It is now that the countdown starts: the future is no longer infinite, it is simply the time they have left. They stop wanting to go faster, their one desire becomes to slow down.

Jean and Laurent would have been astonished if anyone had reminded them that, just ten years earlier, they had talked about Geneviève every day.

Although they still loved each other, their love was less of a miracle now, more of a habit. Each man wondered what his life would have been like if he had made a different choice, if he hadn't selected this particular companion, preferring him over everyone else . . . Naturally, these dizzying questions remained unanswered, but they still cast a shadow over their daily lives.

Jean had stopped listening to Angela's gossip, especially as she had moved from Rue des Renards and had new neighbors.

One day, as he was arranging some items in the window, he had what he thought at first was a vision. On the other side of the glass, a woman with a familiar face was pointing out a lapis lazuli bracelet to a good-looking ten-year-old boy. Jean was so surprised to see Geneviève again, looking impish and bright-eyed in the full bloom of motherhood, and so delighted to see how handsome her son was, that at first he was not sure who to look at, the mother or the child.

David and Geneviève had been strolling in the gallery and

had stopped to look at the jewelry on display in the window, unaware that Jean was watching them from inside the shop.

David's good looks overwhelmed him.

The two window shoppers went on their way. Jean should have gone out, caught up with them, and asked them to come in and have a look at the items that interested them, maybe try them on . . . But he stood there petrified, unable to react. It was as if the shop window had become an uncrossable border, a wall between past and present.

At dinner, when he told Laurent what had happened, his lover teased him gently. "Is this David really so good-looking?"

"Yes, he really is."

The next day, Laurent asked again, "Is David good-looking?"

Jean again said yes, and did his best to describe him.

And the next day, Laurent returned to the same question. "Very good-looking? How exactly?"

Laurent was now questioning him several times an hour . . .

Jean sensed that he wasn't supplying the expected answer. "Do you want to see him?" he suggested. "Why don't we go and wait for him outside his building?"

Laurent almost jumped for joy.

By half past four, they were sitting in their car, which they had parked in the Marolles, on Rue Haute, just above the narrow street where Geneviève lived.

Suddenly the boy appeared and Jean pointed to him.

He had a school satchel on his back, and was not so much walking as dancing along the street, his body as light as his mood.

Laurent leaned forward to get a better look at the boy. Eyes wide open, holding his breath, he turned red as he gazed at him.

Sensing the depth of his friend's emotion, Jean turned to him, and was astounded to see that the veins stood out on his neck.

Smiling, the boy crossed the street, turned onto Rue des Renards, and walked—or rather, jumped—into his building.

Laurent caught his breath. "I'm sure that if you'd had a son, he would have looked like David."

It was at that moment that Jean realized how deep was Laurent's love for him.

They sat there for a long time, their fingers intertwined, resting the backs of their necks against the headrests, their eyes misting over. The emotion they felt was a mixture: partly the strength of their affection for one another, but also the frustration, the intense, deep-seated regret that they had not had children.

"Do you really miss it?" Jean asked.

"A child?"

"Yes. What I miss is a little you, a miniature you, a pocket Jean who would need me, who I could cherish unreservedly, without taking anything away from you. I have a lot of love to give, you know, I have plenty more where this came from." Laurent smiled, relieved at having expressed what he was feeling. "What about you?"

Jean did not reply. He had never put these dreams and disappointments into words, let alone words like those. He kicked the ball into touch. "Are you really so sentimental, my dear Laurent?"

"You attack me instead of answering me. What about you?"

Jean remained silent, and Laurent repeated, as if addressing someone who was hard of hearing, "What about you?"

"I . . . I just can't think the same way you do. It would be like bemoaning my lot, complaining about being gay . . ."

"Is everything still all right?"

"No, but I act as if it is."

"Deep down, you agree with me. Say it! Say you're jealous of all those straight men who can have children just like that, even when they don't love the woman! Say you'd like to have a child running between our legs, a kid who'd take after the two of us. Say it, go on, say it!"

Jean sustained Laurent's gaze. Slowly, almost reluctantly, his eyes agreed. Immediately, he felt them fill with tears, and without understanding why, he began sobbing. Laurent drew Jean's head to his chest, encouraging him to let himself go.

It was a bittersweet moment . . .

When they recovered, Laurent grabbed the wheel. "It's a good thing the boy didn't see us!" he said with a smile. "He would have had a good laugh to see these two old queens blubbering away . . ."

*

From that day on, David became the luckiest boy in the Marolles. Walking on the street, he would find banknotes on the sidewalk. When he was not being randomly chosen for free cinemas tickets, he would receive invitations to the theater sent by some obscure charitable association promoting cultural activities for young people. What letter box was filled with so many free copies—discs, books, scents—as his? The postman would leave gifts, supposedly from the local council, on the doorstep: a bicycle, a tennis racket, roller skates. In the spring, he even won a vacation in Greece—supposedly paid for by two anonymous sponsors who had been impressed by his school grades—and was allowed to take one other person with him. Naturally, he chose his mother. His luck became legendary. He already had plenty of friends because of his lively personality, but now he became *the* person to hang out with because of his good luck. He was equally in demand by adults, who would ask him for his favorite numbers before playing the lottery.

In June, along with some thirty of his friends, David made

his first communion. In the spacious Notre-Dame-de-la-Chapelle, the church of Polish immigrants, Jean and Laurent found themselves surrounded by so many adults—parents, uncles, cousins—celebrating those young people dressed in virginal white that they did not need to hide. They sat down in the front row and were able to gaze at David for a whole hour.

From now on, not a day went by that they did not think about David. Laurent had left the Théâtre Royal du Parc and was now stage manager at the Salle des Galeries, a little chocolate box of a theater specializing in drawing room comedies. As the shop was only some twenty yards from the theater he would often join Jean at L'Atout coeur when he had a break. They would have a drink, talk about this and that—including David—then go back to work.

One afternoon, as they were sampling the tea a female friend had brought back from Japan, the bell at the door tinkled and they sat there stunned, teaspoons in their hands.

David had just come in.

He was fifteen, with curly brown hair, lips the color of raspberries, and a voice that was torn between the sharpness of childhood and the depth of the adult, like a pebble bouncing from head to chest.

"Hello," he said, shutting the door behind him.

Caught in the act—but what act?—Jean and Laurent were unable to either move or speak.

Undaunted, David came closer and gave them a smile that lit up the whole shop. "I'm looking for a gift."

Jean and Laurent were still looking at him wide-eyed.

"Mother's Day is coming up."

Making a huge effort to regain his composure, Jean nodded solemnly, as if he belonged to the select few who knew that Mother's Day would be celebrated in two weeks' time.

Reassured that he had at least gotten some reaction, David went on, "Mom loves your shop."

Hearing this "your," which he had clearly addressed to both of them, Jean and Laurent turned bright red.

Laurent seemed to wake up. "Oh, it isn't my shop, it's his, it's Jean's."

Jean looked at his lover in surprise. Why had he said that? There was no need. What was Laurent implying? That they weren't a couple? Was he trying to make the boy think he was straight?

Jean was so angry, he was about to demand an explanation, but Laurent stopped him dead with a glare and said in a commanding tone, "You see to the young man. I'll finish my tea."

Realizing that he had forgotten David, Jean pulled himself together and turned to the boy. "Tell me what your mother might like," he said, gesturing to David to accompany him around the shop and examine the display cases.

Laurent sat down to contemplate the newcomer. David expressed himself clearly, in well-turned sentences, as he explained what he liked and disliked. He had neither the clumsiness nor the shyness nor the casualness that afflict certain teenage boys. He was self-confident, and easily created a connection with those around him.

As he took out rings, chains and earrings and showed them to the boy, Jean realized why Laurent had said what he had: he had been sensitive enough to yield him the privilege of talking with David.

At the same time, Laurent had given himself the opportunity to observe the two of them together.

Suddenly David gave a start on seeing the tiny label hanging from the clasp of a bracelet that attracted him.

"Is that the price?"

The figure on the label was double what his mother earned in a month.

"No, that's not the price," Jean replied, as quick as a flash. "It's the serial number of the item."

"Really?" David said, half-reassured.

"Once you've chosen, I'll check in my book to see the price corresponding to the number."

Still doubtful that he had enough money, David insisted in a shaky voice, "How much is this bracelet, for example?"

Jean walked to his desk. "What kind of budget do you have for your gift?" he asked casually.

David went pale, swallowed, then stammered, conscious of how ridiculous he must seem, "Fifty?"

With a professional flourish, Jean opened his address book, pretended to look for a number, then said, "Fifty? You have room for maneuver. That costs half—twenty-five."

"Twenty-five?" David said, his voice high-pitched now: he could hardly believe his luck.

"Yes. Twenty-five. And, seeing as it's your first purchase here, I can give you a slight discount. Let's say twenty-two. But that's as low as I can go. Take it or leave it, young man, twenty-two."

David's eyes shone.

Jean and Laurent exchanged a knowing glance: the bracelet was worth forty times that, but neither of them would have admitted it, even under torture.

Jean rejoined David. "Take your time, don't decide straight away. Look, I'll keep my book open, just tell me what you like and I'll tell you the price."

"Oh, thank you, monsieur," David exclaimed, casting a new eye on all these marvels that had suddenly become accessible. He resumed his inspection with renewed gusto.

Jean did not take his eyes off him. "Does your mother collect jewelry?" he asked.

"Oh, no," David replied. "Whenever she has a little money, she spends it on us. She never thinks of herself."

"What about your father?"

The question came from Laurent, still sitting in the shadows, unable to stop himself from asking it.

David turned. "My father's disabled, monsieur. He'd like to take care of us but he's confined to a wheelchair. He can hardly speak."

"Do you love him?"

David stiffened indignantly. "Of course, monsieur. Poor Dad. He may not have had much luck, but at least I do."

Jean and Laurent were silent for several minutes. In the world as David saw it, Eddy was his real father, Eddy loved him, Eddy adored his wife, Eddy would have worked hard if he hadn't been struck down. Such touching innocence melted the hearts of the two men. As far as they were concerned, the boy was no ordinary teenager, he was an angel fallen among devils.

After half an hour, David found himself faced with a dilemma: he was torn between the famous bracelet and a pair of emerald earrings. The two lovers stared at each other, blushing slightly, their temples throbbing. They both hoped that David would choose the emeralds, which were the most expensive item in the shop. There was such a discrepancy between the real price and the price he would pay, the mere thought of it filled them with glee. Now that was a lie that would have a bit of flair!

"I wonder . . . " David murmured.

"Yes?"

"Are these emeralds?"

Jean wanted to help the boy, not take advantage of him. Especially as he wasn't stupid. "You're right, young man. At that price, you won't get emeralds. Mind, though, they aren't fake emeralds made of glass either! If you hit them, they'd withstand the blow."

"Really?" David stammered, intrigued.

"Yes. It's a semi-precious stone from Brazil that's meant as a substitute for emeralds. It's called emerodino. To look at, to touch, it'd fool anyone, even professionals. You'd have to do a chemical analysis to detect the difference. I prefer not to lie to you."

"Thank you."

"That doesn't mean you can't tell your mother they're emeralds."

"Oh, no! She'd never understand how I could afford them."

"As you wish."

When David left, his treasure in his hand, after thanking the two men profusely, as if aware that he owed them a lot, Jean and Laurent collapsed into the armchairs, exhausted.

"Just imagine! He came in . . ."

"He spoke to us . . . "

"David!"

"Congratulations on inventing the emerodino! I almost fell for it myself."

Laurent stood up and looked out at the Galerie de la Reine, which still bore traces of David in the air, then looked at Jean. "If anything happens to us, Jean, I'd like everything we have to go to David."

Jean sat up. "What?"

"Imagine we're on a plane," Laurent went on, "and the captain informs us there's a technical fault that can't be remedied. Well, before we crashed, we'd at least have two consolations. One, we'd be dying together, two, we'd make David rich."

"I agree with you two hundred percent."

The following day, they went to their lawyer and drew up two identical wills. Each bequeathed everything to the remaining member of the couple, but if both men were dead, the inheritance would go to David Grenier.

That night, they opened three bottles of champagne, made several toasts to that child who was not there and suspected nothing, and made love until dawn.

*

Every year, David came back to the shop just before Mother's Day. He was a man now, but had kept the liveliness and freshness of a child, which made him not only admirable but touching.

Every year, David saw these two men, thinking he had not seen them for a year, unaware that they had been watching him. School outings, sporting activities, plays—none of his public appearances had escaped Jean and Laurent, who would slip into the crowd without David or Geneviève ever noticing them.

They forbade themselves to do more. Their attachment to David and Geneviève had to remain secret, like their wedding behind the pillar in Sainte-Gudule thirty-five years earlier. True, there was an occasion when David expressed an interest in the theater, and Laurent offered to take him backstage. But the next time something like that happened—Jean had suggested taking the boy to a classic movie that was showing nearby—Laurent fortunately intervened: there was no question of forging ties of friendship with David! They might be keeping track of his life, but they had to remain apart.

At the age of eighteen, David got enough money together to buy himself a secondhand motorcycle. The two lovers shuddered, fearing he might have an accident. Every evening, they would drive through Rue des Renards, where the Greniers lived, to make sure that the bike was there, intact, tied to a bench not far from the entrance, and as soon as they spotted the blue bodywork they would sigh with relief.

The thing they could never have foreseen happened one Tuesday in November.

Opening their newspaper to the local news page, they learned that a drunken brawl had broken out in the rough area near the Gare du Midi, a brawl that had left two people wounded and one dead. The dead person was an innocent bystander, a high school student riding a motorbike.

Jean and Laurent turned pale. Could it be David?

As the item did not mention the name, they jumped straight into their car. Of course, on the ride to the Marolles, they laughed at their own panic, kept telling themselves that there were dozens, even hundreds of young men who rode motorcycles. But their nonchalance was feigned—what they really felt was an awful, nagging premonition that something terrible had happened to David.

They were right. When they reached the building, not only was the motorcycle not there, but the neighbors were laying flowers along the wall.

David had died when his bike had skidded as he had tried to avoid the fight.

*

Rarely had so much genuine grief been seen at a funeral service. David had been idolized: everyone who had met him—whatever their age or sex—had fallen under his spell and found it hard to accept that he was gone.

Johnny, Minnie, Claudia—his brother and sisters—were trying hard to put on a brave face. At the end of their tether, red-eyed, their features haggard, they would have liked to be alone with their grief: living it in public was a kind of desecration. Luckily, their understanding spouses looked after the children—David's nephews and nieces, shattered at the loss of their young uncle—and welcomed the guests.

Geneviève was not crying. She sat as pale and stiff as a marble statue, staring into the distance, above people's heads. It was as if everything had died in her. She showed no emotion, looked nobody in the face, and replied to the condolences mechanically, as if she had sent an automaton in her place.

At the end of the row, next to the harmonium, Eddy sat huddled in his wheelchair. His face was completely expressionless. Was he grief-stricken, or pleased that this false son who wasn't even his had finally gone? His true thoughts lay hidden within his crippled body.

Jean and Laurent managed to maintain their dignity during the service, but broke down when the coffin was lifted. To think that David, their David, young, handsome David, was lying lifeless in the wooden box being carried through the church by his friends . . . Pushing back their chairs, they rushed out, reaching the front steps before the cortège, ran to their car and drove home, where they took refuge, closing the shutters to give free rein to their despair.

*

The two men had changed.

Up until now fate had spared them, but after the scandal of David's death they relaxed their vigilance. They did nothing to hold back the wrinkles, the white hair, the sadness. They aged overnight.

Their lives had become meaningless.

Reaching the age of sixty, Laurent, having lost interest in his profession, took early retirement.

As often happens, this sudden cessation of activity proved fatal. He complained of discomfort, then of shooting pains. Finally, a medical examination revealed that he had multiple sclerosis, a disease whose worst characteristic is that it can develop in various unpredictable ways. Laurent knew he was doomed, but did not know if he had one year or twenty left to live.

At the beginning of his martyrdom, he would join Jean in the shop, and make an effort to help him. But eventually the pain made it impossible for him to move. First he was given crutches. Then a wheelchair was ordered for him.

When the chair was delivered to Avenue Lepoutre, Laurent exclaimed venomously, "Well, Jean, you once wondered how you would react if your love was put to the test, now you're going to find out."

Jean went to Laurent and placed a finger on his mouth. "It's a test for you, not for me. I'm not forcing myself to take care of you, I'm not making any sacrifices, I love you."

Laurent, unable to bear being diminished like that or the way other people looked at him, became aggressive, picked quarrels with the friends who visited him, drove everyone away then, like a petulant child, complained of being alone. Biting, wounding, killing with words was the last power he had left, the last proof of his virility. The only thing in him that was getting any stronger was his anger.

Jean had the idea of buying a house in Provence. That would allow them to get away, to enjoy the sun, the country-side . . . even find some peace, perhaps? He purchased an eighteenth-century residence in gilded stone, installed a manager in his shop in Brussels, and moved to France with Laurent.

When Laurent died, one Christmas Eve, Jean's first thought was to kill himself. Then, standing by the glittering tree, around which lay gifts that would never be opened, he thought of the people who would have to be informed, the funeral arrangements that would have to be made, all their affairs that needed settling . . . It would be cowardly to just slip away and leave strangers to deal with such thankless tasks! Out of respect for these strangers, he put off his suicide.

He returned to Brussels with Laurent's body, purchased two lots in the cemetery at Ixelles, and arranged a simple ceremony.

At the lawyer's office, the old fellow insisted on reading a document Jean had hoped he would never have to hear: Laurent's will. As he already knew, Laurent had left everything to him. The lawyer took the opportunity of his visit to advise

him to make a new will of his own. The existing one was out of
date, given that the two people it mentioned—Laurent and
David—were both dead.

Jean thought about this. These last few years, during which he
had hidden the gravity of Laurent's condition, had isolated him
from his friends and colleagues, his former customers, his distant
relatives. Nobody had been there to share his ordeal. Who had
been generous to him? Who should he be generous to?

He had several ideas, all possible, none tempting. Finally,
exhausted, he was about to ask the lawyer to suggest some
charities when an image came back to him: the image of
Geneviève leaving the hospital, pushing her paralyzed Eddy in
his wheelchair. She knew what he had been through! She had
been through it herself! Hadn't she devoted her time to a disabled man, hadn't she lost loved ones—her Giuseppe who had
returned to a self-imposed exile in Italy, and above all her
David? *Her* David? *Their* David . . . Laurent had loved him so
much . . .

He burst out laughing.

The lawyer thought he was feeling dizzy.

"Are you all right, Monsieur Daemens?"

"Perfectly all right."

Since, in Laurent's eyes, David had been Jean's child symbolically, why shouldn't Jean regard Geneviève as the mother
of his son?

"There's a woman I was more or less married to once. I'd
like to leave everything to her."

And so Jean dictated the will that transformed Geneviève
Grenier, maiden name Piastre, who had married in Sainte-
Gudule Cathedral one April 13, into his sole heir.

*

After that, he decided to let himself die.

Alas, his good health kept him alive. There was nothing he could do about it. Sadness, boredom and revulsion were enough to ruin his life, not to end it. Idly reading classic novels, he envied the old days when people died of sorrow. Madame de Clèves languished away, so did Balzac's heroines . . . Not him. But then they were women. Did they suffer more than men? Was it his gender that stopped him from dying of emotion?

After five aimless years, he at last took to his bed with a bad case of flu. Determined as well as meticulous, he made sure he did not call the doctor until it was too late.

When he sensed that his time was almost up, he closed his eyes and thought about Laurent. Deep inside him, something still remained of the Catholic faith of his childhood, and he hoped that what he had once been taught was true: he would soon be reunited with the man he loved . . .

He passed away with a confident smile on his lips.

* * *

From the balcony of her apartment, Geneviève gazed down at the lawns and pink sandy paths of the elegant avenue where the globular street lamps stood out against the chestnut trees. In their linen suits, residents were walking their dogs, rare pedigree breeds that paraded nonchalantly, as stylish as their masters. Geneviève had just moved to 22 Avenue Lepoutre. Was "moved" the right word, when this apartment contained ten times more furniture than the van had brought from the Marolles?

Her children would be here soon, and she still hadn't solved the mystery of her benefactor.

In his houses, Jean had burned the documents, letters and

photograph albums that might have told her something about his life. She hadn't been able to learn much through gossip either, because the building no longer had a concierge, and a firm of interchangeable Turkish workers had taken care of maintenance for the past ten years. Moreover, the former neighbors had moved, and the new ones had caught mere glimpses of a solitary old man. The few clues she had gleaned added up to a confused and discouraging story. According to some, Jean was a misanthrope, according to others he had carried on a mysterious affair with a married woman, while others still had an even more absurd version: that he'd had a homosexual relationship with the man whose grave she had seen next to his. People can be so wicked . . . She couldn't imagine a virile man like the one she had seen in that photograph in the arms of a boy . . .

The doorbell rang. Her children were arriving.

She was going to have to come up with an explanation.

Minnie was the first. No sooner had she given her mother a hug than she began walking admiringly around the apartment. Five minutes later, Johnny and Claudia arrived. They at least went to the trouble of having an innocuous conversation with her to start, but then also launched into an exploration of the premises.

"I've made tea and had a cake delivered," Geneviève announced.

At the words "had a cake delivered," she sensed a tension in the air, and realized that she had started to sound like a rich woman.

Once seated around the table, they looked at her, an identical question in their eyes.

"Yes, I won't hide it from you, my dears, I was left a lot."

And as her children listened in amazement, she listed the possessions and real estate that she now owned. It was her way of demonstrating her good faith, of showing them that she was holding nothing back. In reality, she was preparing the ground for what was to come.

Impressed, they fidgeted impatiently in their chairs.

Then she cut the raspberry gateau, a local specialty, and served the tea. She hoped this would provide a few moments' respite, but it was not to be.

"But why?" Minnie cried.

"Why what?" said Geneviève with difficulty.

"Why did the man leave you all this?"

She studied the three faces in front of her. From their expressions, she could guess the answer they already carried within them. Of course, like everyone with whom she had brought up the subject, they assumed she had been Jean Daemens's mistress, the only theory anyone found credible. She was going to have to fight, to justify herself, to convince them to accept something inconceivable, a pure mystery.

Pushing her cup away, she sat back in her high-backed chair.

"I'm not going to lie to you."

They were staring at her, openmouthed, willing her to say the words.

Without understanding what was happening inside her, she heard herself say, "Jean Daemens was my lover. Yes, Jean Daemens was the love of my life."

Shocked, she said to herself, "Forgive me, Giuseppe."

They were waiting, so she continued, "We loved each other very much. I was going to tell you twenty-five years ago, I was going to introduce him to you and announce that Eddy and I were separating, and then . . . your father became sick. I didn't have the heart to leave, I made up my mind to take care of him . . ."

Much to her own surprise, her voice was shaking. Telling this story moved her. Was it because there were so many truths hidden beneath the lies?

Minnie put her hand indulgently on her mother's and asked in a calm but sad voice, "Mom, why didn't you tell us this after Dad died?"

"Jean didn't want it."

"Why?"

"It was very hard for him."

"Because he'd lost you?"

"It was more than that."

Geneviève's ears were burning: she knew what she was about to say and could hardly believe it. Her lips stammered the words, "Jean was your brother David's father. He never got over his death."

Then she was choked with sobs and was unable to continue. What was the point, anyway?

Her children rushed to embrace her, to kiss her, to reassure her. She did not usually reveal her feelings like this, and they were not only stunned by their mother's secret, but overcome by the depth of her emotion.

Geneviève Grenier, dry-eyed Geneviève, who hadn't shed a tear since David's death, Geneviève Grenier, maiden name Piastre, who had married Eddy Grenier fifty-five years earlier, on the afternoon of April 13 in Sainte-Gudule Cathedral, let herself go, protected by her own deception. She wept at last for her wasted life, her lost love, and the son that death had taken from her.

THE DOG

In memory of Emmanuel Lévinas

For several decades, Samuel Heymann had been the doctor of this village in the Hainaut, much appreciated as a practitioner in spite of his austere demeanor. At the age of seventy, he had unscrewed the brass plaque on his gate and informed the villagers that he would no longer be treating them. In spite of their protests, Samuel Heymann had refused to change his mind: he was retiring, and his neighbors would now have to travel three miles to Mettet, where a competent, newly trained young colleague had just settled. For half a century, nobody had had any complaints about Dr. Heymann, but nobody really knew him.

When I settled in the village, all I was able to find out about him was that after his wife's death, he had raised his daughter by himself, and that he had always lived with the same dog.

"The same one?" I asked in some astonishment.

"Yes, *monsieur*, the same," replied the owner of the Pétrelle, the only café, which was situated opposite the church. "A Beauceron."

Not knowing if he was pulling my leg, I cautiously said, "A Beauceron usually lives . . . ten or twelve years."

"Dr. Heymann has owned a Beauceron called Argos for more than forty years. That's how old I am, and I can confirm that I've always seen them together. If you don't believe me, ask the old-timers."

He pointed to four craggy-faced old men, slim beneath their vast tartan shirts, playing cards beside the TV set.

When he saw my astonished expression, he burst out laughing. "I'm joking, monsieur. What I meant was that Dr. Heymann has stayed loyal to the same breed. Every time one of his Beaucerons dies, he buys a new one and calls it Argos. At least he can be sure he won't get the name wrong when he yells at it."

"How lazy can you be?!" I exclaimed, upset at having been taken for an idiot.

"Lazy?" he grunted, wiping the zinc counter with his cloth. "Hardly the word I'd use to describe Dr. Heymann."

In the months that followed, I was able to ascertain how right he was. The doctor was anything but lazy! In fact, the man never relaxed: at the age of eighty, he still walked his dog several hours a day, cut his own wood, ran a number of associations, and maintained the vast garden of his ivy-covered bluestone manor house. Beyond this rather grand building, the houses stopped and there were just fields and meadows and groves, stretching all the way to the distant forest of Tournibus, a dark, green line on the horizon. This frontier location, on the borderline between the village and the woods, suited Samuel Heymann, a man who moved in two worlds, the human world and the animal world, chatting with his fellow villagers then setting off in the company of his dog for long walks together.

When you saw them at a bend in the path, their appearance was striking: two country gentlemen moving toward you, rustic but elegant, one on two legs, the other on four, similar in size and bearing, both proud and solidly built, treading the soil with confidence, powerful, well-balanced. Whenever another walker appeared, they glared at him, but their looks turned benevolent as soon as the distance was reduced. When you tried to find the differences between the man and his dog, you found only more symmetries: while one dressed in velvet or tweed and the other made do with a thick but short-haired coat, they both wore gloves, the first for real, the second

because nature had given him fawn-colored mittens; Samuel
Heymann had black eyebrows in a pale face, while Argos's eyes
were underlined with beige marks against his black fur, this
contrast being highly expressive in both cases; and these proud
creatures both sported identically strong chests, the master
covering his with a scarf, the quadruped displaying an amber
patch on his.

At first, we were nodding acquaintances, but far from
friends. Since I loved going on long walks with my three dogs,
I often ran into them on those Saturdays and Sundays when I
took refuge in the country.

Samuel Heymann was content at first with a mere nod of
the head, just for custom's sake, although his dog was friend-
lier toward my dogs. After five or six of these encounters,
given that I insisted on exchanging a few words, he agreed to
a little cautious conversation, the kind one stranger engages in
with another, without venturing anything that might denote
familiarity. When he became warmer, thanks to Argos being
so delighted with my Labradors, I thought I had won. But
when I greeted him in the village without my dogs, he didn't
even remember me: his way of perceiving the world starting
with the animal rather than the human, it was my animals he
remembered and liked being with, while I was just an indistinct face floating above the three leashes. This was confirmed
one day when I hurt myself doing some odd job or other and
the owner of the café took me straight to the elderly doctor's.
When Samuel Heymann bent over me and asked me where it
hurt, I had the impression that he was addressing the pain
rather than me, that I had dissolved into the case I repre-
sented, that he was dealing with my problem out of moral
necessity rather than out of sympathy. His regulation philan-
thropy, meticulous and inflexible, reeked of duty, not spontaneity; it was an expression of the will, and that made it
intimidating.

Nevertheless, as the months passed, in spite of a few failures, he did finally begin to recognize me independently of my dogs. Then, when he found out that I was a writer, he opened his door to me.

Our relationship began on a footing of great respect. He liked my books, I loved his modesty.

I invited him to my house, he received me in his. A bottle of whiskey served as a pretext ever since we had discovered a mutual passion for this drink. Sitting by the fire, we would talk about the proportion of malt that gave the precious liquid taste, the process of drying in a peat fire, the essence of the wood the cask was made from; Samuel went so far as to prefer distilleries located by the sea, claiming that as whiskey aged it became imbued with the smells of seaweed, iodine, and salt. Our liking for whiskey had paradoxically developed our taste for water, for, in order to preserve the strongest specimens, single casks of 55 or 60 degrees, we would have two glasses in our hands—one of whiskey, one of water—which led our taste buds to seek out the best springs.

Whenever I entered the room where Samuel Heymann sat in the company of his dog, I always had the feeling I was disturbing them. There they were, man and beast, motionless, beautiful, noble, shrouded in silence, united by the white light filtering in through the curtains. Whatever the hour when I surprised them, they would both have identical expressions, whether pensive, playful or weary . . . As soon as I crossed the threshold, my entrance disturbed their pose and forced the tableau to come to life. The dog would lift his head in surprise, tilt his bald cranium to the left, push his ears forward, then look me up and down with his hazel eyes: "What an indiscreet person! I hope you have a good reason." Less brusquely, his master would suppress a sigh, smile, and stammer a courtesy that barely concealed an exasperated "What? Again?" Joined in a constant communion, spending all their days and nights together, they never seemed to tire of one another, enjoying every moment they shared, as if for them there was nothing more perfect in this world than to breathe side by side. Anyone who suddenly appeared was breaking in on something rich and strong and full.

Outside books and whiskey, our conversations quickly languished. Apart from the fact that Samuel had no patience with general topics, he never told me anything personal, any anecdote about his childhood, his youth, or his love life. He was eighty years old, and yet it was if he had been born yesterday. If I ever delivered myself of a confession, he would receive my confidence but would not give me any revelation in return. True, mention of his daughter sometimes altered this mask, because he loved her, loved her success—she ran a law practice in Namur—and made no secret of the fact. But there too, sincere as he was, he made do with conventional phrases. I came to the conclusion that he had never been passionate about anything, and that I was seeing the full extent of his private life when I contemplated the couple he formed with his dog.

Last summer, a series of lecture tours abroad kept me out of the country for several months. On the eve of my departure, he wished, with a touch of mockery, "A happy journey to the writer who is more interested in talking than in writing." As for me, I promised to bring him back a few valuable books and some rare bottles to occupy our winter.

*

I returned to some devastating news.

A week earlier, the dog Argos had been run over by a truck.

And five days later, Samuel had taken his own life.

The village was in a state of shock. In a tearful voice, the grocer told me the news before I got home: the doctor's housekeeper had found him lying on the floor of his kitchen, pieces of brain and blood spattering the tiled walls. According to the police, he had taken his rifle and shot himself in the mouth.

"Magnificent . . . " I thought.

We never react to a death the way we are expected to: instead of feeling sadness, I was weak with admiration.

My first impulse was to revere that spectacular, grandiose, logical comclusion: Samuel and his dog had been a couple to the end! That double death struck me as flagrantly romantic. There was no doubt that the death of one had called for the death of the other. And as was their wont, they had acted in concert, abandoning life almost simultaneously, both suffering a violent demise.

Then I recovered my self-control and reprimanded myself for my thoughts: *Don't be ridiculous. No one's ever killed himself because his dog was run over by a car. Samuel may have been planning suicide for ages, but put it off as long as he did in order to take care of his companion. Once the dog was gone, he carried out his plan . . . Or maybe, just after Argos's accident, Samuel learned that he was suffering from an incurable illness, and wanted to spare himself a long, drawn-out death . . . Yes, yes, it must be something like that . . . A series of coincidences! He didn't kill himself for grief. No one's ever committed suicide because his dog was run over.*

The more I denied that hypothesis, the more sensible and self-evident it seemed.

Irritably, my head heavy, I decided not to go straight home but headed instead for the Pétrelle, just to pay tribute to our friend Samuel by commemorating his memory with my fellow villagers.

Unfortunately, public rumor was even more inflamed than my imagination: at the bar, at the tables, along the broad sidewalk where, in spite of the cold, the regulars had come out to drink their beer, everyone thought that Dr. Heymann had taken his own life because of what had happened to his dog.

"If you'd seen him when he picked the animal up from the road, all in pieces like that . . . It was terrifying."

"He must have been distraught."

"No, he was filled with hatred! He kept screaming 'No!' and spitting at the sky, with his eyes all bloodshot, then he turned to us as we approached him and I really thought he was going to kill us all! I mean we hadn't done anything, but the way he looked at us . . . If he'd had daggers instead of eyes, we'd have all been goners."

"Where was this?"

"The Villers Road, after the Tronchons' farm."

"And who did it?"

"Nobody knows. He drove straight off."

"That dog was clever, though. It avoided cars and never ran away from its master."

"Maryse, his housekeeper, told me they were both looking at mushrooms at the side of the ditch when a truck passed at top speed, missing the doctor by a hair's breadth but hitting Argos full on in the pelvis. The dog was torn to pieces. The truck driver must have seen them, but didn't swerve by an inch to avoid them. A real bastard!"

"There are some stupid people around!"

"Poor animal."

"Poor animal and poor doctor."

"But then to go and blow his brains out afterwards!"

"You can't argue with grief."

"All the same!"

"Dammit, Heymann was a doctor—he'd seen people die before and never killed himself."

"Well, maybe he loved his dog more than he loved people . . ."

"I'm afraid you're right."

"Stop! He'd already lost other dogs. Whenever one of them died, he didn't think twice, he'd just go out and buy a new one. In fact, people were shocked that he didn't wait longer."

"Maybe this Argos was better than the others."

"Or else the doctor was getting tired."

"Hold on a minute! The other dogs all died normally, of old age. Not turned into mincemeat by a hit-and-run driver!"

"All the same, I think it's a bit weird to love dogs so much, and you'll never persuade me otherwise."

"To love dogs so much or people so little?"

After these words, silence fell on the room. The percolator hissed. The television murmured the results of the horse races. A fly, suddenly desperate to attract attention, flattened itself against the wall. Everyone was asking themselves the question: Which is easier to love, a man or a dog? And which is better at returning our love?

It was a disquieting question.

Lost in thought, I walked mechanically back to my house. My Labradors were delighted to see me, leaped in the air, and wagged their tails so enthusastically that their bodies were thrown off balance. As I stroked them, it hit me for a fraction of a second that I didn't give them back as much as they gave me, and that Samuel Heymann, in his passion for Argos, had far surpassed me. That had been pure love, the love of his life . . .

I opened my most expensive bottle of whiskey, an old malt from the island of Islay, the one I had intended for Samuel. That evening, I drank for two.

*

The next day, his daughter Miranda came to see me.

I barely knew her, had only met her two or three times, but had liked her right from the start. She was lively, precise, independent, unaffected, almost abrupt, one of those modern women who charm you by their very refusal to use their charms. Addressing me as a man would have done, in a manner devoid of undertones, she had put me at my ease, so much at ease that subsequently, when I had noticed how fine her features were and how feminine her legs, I felt a surprise tinged with wonder.

Miranda stood there in the morning mist with her shock of red hair, smiled, asked if she was disturbing me, brandished some croissants she had just bought, and suggested a coffee. There was as much naturalness as authority in the way she took control.

As we went into the kitchen, I offered her my condolences, which she received with her head bowed, inscrutable. She sat down facing me.

"My father liked talking with you. Maybe he told you things . . . things he wouldn't have told me."

"We talked mostly about books and whiskey. That was it, really—books and whiskey."

"Sometimes, when people talk about some general subject, they connect it with a specific memory."

I sat down and told her that, in spite of all my efforts, our conversations had never taken a personal turn.

"He was protecting himself," I concluded.

"From what?" Miranda said with exasperation. "Or from whom? I'm his only daughter, I loved him, but I know nothing about him. He always behaved impeccably toward me, but he was always a stranger. That's my one reproach: he did everything for me except tell me who he was." From her basket she took an unwieldy volume. "Look at this."

It was a photograph album, each stiff page protected by silk paper. I leafed through it sadly. It began with the wedding of Samuel and Édith, a pretty redhead with a sweet mouth; at their feet, a Beauceron posed, as proud as if it were the couple's child. Then a baby appeared on the scene—it, too, watched over by the animal. These group photographs showed a smiling family of four, a trio formed by the married couple and the dog, to which the baby was added. When Miranda was five, Édith disappeared.

"What happened to your mother?"

"A brain tumor. She died very quickly."

The photographs now were of a reconstituted family: the dog had taken the wife's place beside its master, and it was Miranda who stood in front of them.

"Do you notice anything?" she asked suddenly.

"Er . . . There are no photographs dating from your father's childhood or adolescence."

"His parents died during the war. Like lots of Jews whose families were murdered, he didn't like to talk about them . . . I don't know anything at all about my grandparents, uncles or aunts. He was the only one who survived."

"How?"

"During the war, he was hidden in a Catholic boarding school in Namur. By a priest. Father . . . André. Don't you notice anything else?"

I sensed where she was trying to lead me. Like me, like the villagers, she was wondering about the importance of the dog, wondering if it was the accident that had led to her father's desperate act. I didn't dare mention the subject myself, assuming that, for a daughter, such a suspicion must be a source of great suffering.

She was staring at me, urgent, demanding, trusting. I finally stammered, "Miranda, what was your relationship with your father's dogs?"

She sighed, relieved that I had finally gone to the heart of the matter. Finishing her coffee, she sat back in her chair and looked at me. "Daddy only ever had one dog at a time. A Beauceron named Argos. I'm fifty now and I knew four of them."

"Why a Beauceron?"

"No idea."

"And why Argos?"

"No idea either."

"And what did you think of them?"

She hesitated, not very accustomed to formulating these feelings, but wanting to do so. "I loved them all. Really loved them. First of all, they were good dogs, lively, affectionate, devoted. And besides, they were my brothers, my sisters . . . " She broke off for a moment to think, then went on, "They were my mother too . . . And my father, a little . . . " Tears welled up in her eyes. She had surprised even herself.

I tried to help her. "Brother or sister, Miranda, that I can understand, because the dog obeyed your father and became your companion. But . . . your mother?"

A faraway look came into her eyes. Although she was staring down at the floor, it was obvious from their opaque stillness that, inside, they were focused on memories.

"Argos understood me better than Daddy did. If I was sad, or angry, or ashamed, Argos would sense it immediately. He knew all my moods. Like a mother . . . He would tell my father. Oh yes, there were lots of times when Argos interceded with Daddy to remind him that he should be paying attention to me, listening to me, getting me to open up. At those moments, when Daddy obeyed him, Argos would sit upright between us, watching both of us, making sure that I was telling my father, in the complicated language of humans, what he, a dog, had immediately grasped."

Her voice had become both softer and more high-pitched, and her hand shook as she put her hair back in place. Without realizing it, Miranda was reverting to the little girl she was talking about.

"And it was Argos that I got all the hugs and kisses from," she went on. "Like a mother . . . Daddy was always very reserved with me. The hours we spent, Argos and I, lying side by side on the carpet, dreaming and talking! His was the only body I touched, and the only body that touched me. Like a mother, don't you think?"

She was questioning me like a lost little girl who wanted confirmation that she was correctly defining what she had lacked.

"Like a mother . . . " I echoed approvingly.

She smiled, reassured. "I had often had Argos's smell on me. Because he'd jump on me. Because he'd lick me. Because he'd cling to my legs. Because he needed to prove his affection. In my childhood, Argos had a smell, and Daddy didn't. He would keep his distance, he didn't smell of anything, or else he smelled clean. I mean, he had a civilized smell, the smell that comes from bottles, eau de cologne or antiseptic, a man's smell, a doctor's smell. Only Argos had a smell all his own. And I had his."

She looked up at me, and I said in her place, "Like a mother . . . "

A long silence followed. I didn't dare break it, guessing that Miranda was remembering all the happy times in her past. She was about to enter a period of mourning. But whom was she mourning? Samuel or Argos?

She must have read my thoughts because the next thing she said was, "I can't think of Daddy without thinking of Argos. One never went without the other. Daddy knew his own limitations, so he relied on his dog to grasp what escaped him. I often had the impression he consulted him, depended on his decisions. Argos was like part of Daddy, the physical part, the empathetic part, the sensitive part. Argos was a little bit my father and my father was a little bit Argos. Does what I'm saying sound crazy?"

"Not at all."

I made some more coffee. We didn't need to talk: we had

reached that degree of calm that we reach not when we have discovered the truth, but when we come close to a mystery.

As I poured the coffee, I asked, "Do you think the last Argos had something more than the previous ones?"

She quivered, grasping that we were approaching the main subject of the day. "He was remarkable and unique. Like his predecessors."

"Did your father love him more?"

"My father was more of a recluse."

We both sat there openmouthed. Each of us wanted to talk, but neither dared.

"Everyone here thinks he killed himself because of the dog," she said at last, looking me straight in the eyes. "Don't they?"

"It's absurd, but . . . yes," I stammered. "Given that we don't have enough information, that we didn't know your father well, we can't help linking the two events."

"He would have hated people to say that."

I almost corrected her by saying, "You hate people to say that." Luckily, a vestige of tact held me back.

She leaned forward. "Help me."

"I'm sorry?"

"Help me to understand what happened."

"Why me?"

"Because Daddy liked you. And because you're a novelist."

"Being a novelist doesn't mean being a detective."

"Being a novelist means being fascinated by other people."

"I don't know anything about your father."

"Your imagination will make up for that. You know, I've read your books, and I've noticed that when you don't know something, you fantasize. I need your genius for hypotheses."

"Hold on a minute! I write what I like because my stories don't have consequences. I'm not looking for truth, just entertainment."

"Why should the truth be any uglier than silence? Help me. Please help me."

Her big green eyes were imploring me, her flaming red hair blazed with anger.

I liked Miranda so much that, without thinking, I agreed.

*

That afternoon, I joined her at her father's house, where we undertook to go through his papers in the hope of finding something.

After two or three futile hours, I exclaimed, "Miranda, your father's dogs all came from the same place. A kennel in the Ardennes."

"What of it?"

"In the last fifty years, the contracts have been signed by one person, a man named—"

At that moment, the doorbell rang. Miranda opened the door to the Comte de Sire, an elderly man in riding boots, dressed with archaic refinement. Behind him, his horse, tied to the gatepost, neighed when it saw us.

His family, which had once owned several farms and three châteaux, now lived on an estate some seven miles away.

He had come to offer his condolences, and was hopping from foot to foot, red-faced with embarrassment.

Miranda showed him in and indicated one of the high arm-chairs that formed a semicircle in front of the fireplace in the drawing room. He stepped forward humbly, looked around the room, and thanked her in a muffled voice, as if she had allowed him to enter the holy of holies.

"Your father was . . . an exceptional man. I've never in my life known anyone else who was so humane, so kind, so perceptive about other people and their misfortunes. He grasped everything without explanation. He was truly gifted with enormous compassion."

Miranda and I exchanged looks of surprise. Although we

would have liked to boast of Samuel Heymann's qualities, those weren't the ones we would have chosen, because, in our opinion, he didn't have them.

"Did he ever mention me?" the Comte de Sire asked Miranda.

She made a face as she searched in her memory. "No."

The count blushed and smiled: this omission was yet more evidence of the dead man's virtues.

"Were you friends?" Miranda asked.

"I wouldn't say that. Let's put it this way: I'd done everything to be his enemy, but thanks to his generosity of spirit, I wasn't."

"I don't understand."

"We shared secrets. He's taken his with him. I shall soon do the same with mine."

Irritably, Miranda struck the armchair with the flat of her hand. "That's just like my father: a nest of secrets! I can't stand it."

At this violent outburst, the count's lower lip dropped, he foamed a little at the mouth, his eyelashes fluttered, then he emitted a few rumbling noises that were meant as words of comfort to Miranda, although he was not very good at comforting.

She went up to him. "Does this have any connection with my mother?"

"I'm sorry?"

"Your quarrel with him! The thing he forgave you! Was it to do with my mother?"

"No, not at all," he hissed, conclusively. He was offended that Miranda could have thought such a thing. In his eyes, she had crossed the threshold of vulgarity.

"Don't you have anything else to tell me?" Miranda insisted.

The man fiddled with the gloves he had laid across his knees and coughed two or three times. "Yes!"

"Well?"

"I'd like to pay my respects to your father. Will you allow me to arrange his funeral?"

"What?"

"I'd like to offer him a ceremony worthy of him, noble, dignified. Let me spend some money, organize the ceremony, put flowers in the church, bring singers and an orchestra, hire a luxurious hearse drawn by horses from my stable."

He was already in a rapture over the scenes he was imagining.

Miranda threw me a glance that meant, "This old bird is crazy." Then she shrugged. "I should answer: Why? But I'm going to say: Why not? Agreed! Organize away, monsieur, I'll provide the corpse."

The man raised an eyebrow, shocked by Miranda's insolence. But he refrained from reacting and contented himself, as he walked back to the front door, with thanking her profusely.

Once he had left us, Miranda gave free rein to her astonishment. "The Comte de Sire! He shows up and behaves like his best friend, even though Daddy never mentioned his name to me! Secrets . . . Nothing but secrets."

I returned to the documents I was holding in my hand. "Miranda, I insist. If I were you, I'd go to the kennel where your father chose his dogs for the past fifty years."

"Why?"

"I suspect he was capable of telling a Beauceron breeder what he hid from you."

"All right. When do we leave?"

*

After three hours' driving, we hit the Ardennes. The roads wound through windswept forests. Houses became sparser, and we had the feeling we were entering a world apart, a purely vegetable world. The spruces, their trunks attacked by fierce lichen, were neither high nor close together, but they stood there in numberless ranks, forming an impenetrable mass, like an army ready to attack. Their branches were heavy with rain and drooped low over our car. I dreaded breaking down in this hostile region.

At last we got to the kennels of Bastien and Sons. Surrounded by the sounds of barking coming from several buildings, we had difficulty in persuading the young man who had approached our vehicle that we didn't want to buy a pedigree dog, or leave one there, but only to see Monsieur François Bastien, who for fifty years had sold Beaucerons to Miranda's father.

"I'll take you to my grandfather," he said, skeptically.

We entered a low-ceilinged room, its walls laden with brass pans. The tables were strewn with embroidered doilies and pewterware, a veritable treasure trove for an antique dealer, a heap of old bric-a-brac to Miranda and me.

François Bastien, the dog master, came toward us. When we had explained the situation, he offered Miranda his condolences and invited us to sit down.

Miranda admitted to him that coming here might seem bizarre, but she loved her father and knew too little about him. Could he help her?

"My God, the first time I met your dad was after the war. He'd just lost his dog. He showed me a photograph of it so that I could find a Beauceron that looked like it. It wasn't difficult."

"Do you think he'd always had a dog? That they were fond of Beaucerons in his family?"

I had started, without realizing it, to put together various hypotheses, trying to give his behavior some logic: the Beauceron might have been the element that linked the orphan to his past, symbolizing that lost connection. Hence his irrational attachment . . .

François Bastien destroyed my speculations immediately. "Oh, no, the Beauceron he'd just lost was his first dog, I'm certain of that. At that time, Monsieur Heymann knew as much about animals as I knew about knitting, and I had to give him advice."

I modified my theory. "Was it the dog he'd adopted when he was hidden?"

"Hidden?"

"Yes, my father was hidden in a Catholic boarding school during the war," Miranda said.

The man rubbed his chin, producing a dry, rasping sound. "Hidden? That's strange . . . I was sure he'd been a prisoner."

"I beg your pardon?"

"A prisoner."

"Did he tell you that?"

"No. Now, how did I get that idea in my head?" The weary-looking François Bastien searched in his memories. "Oh, yes! It was because of the photograph. The photograph of him with his dog. In it, he was wearing a kind of uniform. And there was barbed wire in the background. Yes, that's it, barbed wire." He sighed. "When I first met him, your father was just starting to study medicine. Frankly, all credit to him, because he didn't have a cent, and at the time it was hard to get food if you didn't have a family in the country. He worked as a night watchman to pay for his studies. At first, I refused to sell him the dog: he wanted to spread the payment over several months! 'Don't buy an animal,' I told him. 'It's hard enough for you to feed yourself. Plus, a Beauceron's a big eater. Better to keep the old one in a photograph in your pocket than feed a new one.' You know what he said? 'If I don't get another dog, I'll die.'"

Miranda shuddered. She was hearing the words she had hoped not to hear.

"Yes, that's right," the old man went on, engrossed now in

his memories. "'If I don't get another dog, I'll die.' And then he said, 'I'll never manage if I don't have a dog with me.' When he said that, he wasn't all weepy, like some of these old ladies who can't do without a pet, no, he was indignant, angry, as if someone was about to tear out his liver. I felt sorry for him. I agreed to spread out the payment, and I let him have a puppy, which he called Argos. And it turned out I did the right thing: your father became a doctor, he earned a good living, and he remained loyal to my kennel. At the time, I acted out of the goodness of my heart, but it was also a good investment."

"Why Argos?"

"The previous one had been called Argos."

"Is it common for dog owners to do that, to use only one name?"

"No. Apart from Dr. Heymann, I've never met anyone who only called his dogs by one name."

"Why did he do that, in your opinion?"

"God knows! Clearly, his first dog had meant a lot to him."

"And his last," I said. "Dr. Heymann killed himself five days after a truck ran it down."

Bastien sat there openmouthed, his eyes popping out, torn between his desire to condemn a human being capable of such stupidity and his desire to spare Miranda.

We continued the conversation for another twenty minutes, but François Bastien was devoid of anecdotes and couldn't find anything more in his lackluster memory, which was as worn as an old lighter. We thanked him and set off again.

The return journey was long and silent. We were both thinking, both unable to figure out if we should give credence to what Bastien had told us. Samuel Heymann a prisoner? Samuel Heymann giving up on life if he was deprived of his dog at the age of twenty and then at eighty? Far from answering us, these words brought new questions, bewildering doubts . . . The case of Samuel Heymann wasn't getting any clearer, but increasingly obscure.

Miranda and I parted with a few kind words. We each preferred to brood on our disappointment alone.

*

The next day, as I was idly dipping some defrosted, greasy, burned croissants in a cup of coffee, the bell rang.

I thought it was Miranda. It was actually the postman, delivering an intimidating-looking registered letter. I made a face and signed for it, said goodbye to him, and examined the object. Immediately, I shuddered. The sender was Dr. Samuel Heymann.

It had been sent on the third, the day of his suicide. I closed the door and leaned back against it, looking around suspiciously, like a spy dreading to be observed. I had received a message from a dead man! My hands were shaking so much that I was afraid I would tear the contents as I opened the envelope.

Three documents awaited me inside.

A short letter, only one page.

A photograph.

Some sheets of paper stapled together.

I read the letter first:

> Dear writer who talks more than he writes,
>
> I am turning to you because I suffer from two unfortunate infirmities: I possess neither tact nor a gift for writing. But in order to emerge from a silence that has lasted sixty years, I need at least those qualities.
>
> The papers that accompany this note are addressed to my daughter but I'd like you to convey them to her, by reading them aloud and, above all, by improving them. You alone are capable

of giving them a certain grace; I don't know how to go from silence to music. Do it, please, do it for me and for her. The silence I imposed on Miranda was intended to protect her. Breaking it during my lifetime would have amounted to making her vulnerable. Now that I am leaving, this armor will become a burden. Tell her that a father's love is a difficult love because it cannot be content with spontaneity, it has to be more calculating than any other love. I have tried to be a father. With all my strength, with all my intelligence. It is Miranda I'm thinking about before leaving this earth. She is what I am leaving behind me. I am happy to have given the world this miraculous gift, her beauty, her sensitivity, her personality, so radiant, so powerful, so . . . My little girl, I am very proud of you.

The text stopped there, the last lines tilting unsteadily to the right. Emotion must have prevented him from continuing.

Can you conclude with words when, a few minutes later, a gun will have the last word?

In my opinion, at the bottom of that page, Samuel Heymann had not only stopped writing, he had also deliberately stopped feeling. Confessing more might have led him to give up on the idea and remain among us . . . Courage and cowardice are very close, two sides of the same feeling.

I went upstairs to my room, lay down on the bed, and began reading the sheets of paper covered in Samuel Heymann's handwriting:

I often feel as if I never had a childhood. The memories I still have of it belong to someone else. That wasn't me, that affectionate, confident boy, with his arms open, quivering at the splendor of the world, safe in the conviction that he could last forever, outlive the animals, the men, the clouds, the sun, the sea and the plains. In the morning, when he got out of bed, he would run down to the courtyard

*of the building, lift his head, and cry to heaven, "You can
go to bed, God, it's all right, I'm awake now, I'll take care
of everything." No, that wasn't me, the boy who always
found a shoulder to curl up against, who would go to sleep
on his mother's breast, the invincible boy who dreamed
that he would learn music, literature, dancing, painting,
medicine, architecture, and that he would live in a castle.
That all-conquering, optimistic child endowed with an
impatient joy, boosted by the love of his family, that prince
who didn't doubt that he was loved or lovable, was someone else. Not me.*

*Because I only began to exist later. I began with a separa-
tion . . .*

*One day, they came to our house to arrest us. There were
six of us, my grandparents, my parents, my elder sister, and
me.*

*Of course, we should have been more aware of the dangers
threatening us, but, faced with the rise of the Nazis, the grow-
ing anti-Semitism, we Heymanns tended to downplay the
horror of each new development, assuming that "this was the
last one," that "after this, they couldn't go any further." The
reality, alas, could only be brought home to us through violence.*

*In 1942, then, the police came for us. My sister and I were
reading in our room when they knocked at the door. Hearing
the men attack our parents, Rita hid me at the bottom of the
toy chest and covered me with her dolls. "Don't move!" Then,
when the police burst into our room, she ran to the window
and screamed as if I was out on the street, "Run, Samuel, run!
Don't come back to the house! They want to arrest us." They
slapped her to shut her up but fell into her trap: they didn't
bother to check and left me behind.*

*When, an hour later, I resolved to get out of the chest, I
cursed Rita as I walked through the empty apartment. Oh,*

yes, I was free, but what was I to do with this freedom? I would have much preferred being with my family. My wicked sister had deprived me of my parents and grandparents, the selfish girl had kept them for herself and doomed me to solitude. Because I wasn't accustomed to misfortune, I turned my sadness into anger. I punched the furniture, I insulted my absent sister. Overcome with rage, I had forgotten who the real villains were.

Because of the noise I was making, one of our neighbors realized that, in spite of the raid, there was still someone in the Heymanns' apartment. Madame Pasquier came down, found me in tears, sized up the situation, and that very night took me to her cousins in the country.

After that, Miranda, I became that hidden child I briefly—all too briefly—mentioned to you. Hidden at first in several barns, thanks to the resistance network, I was placed under a false name as a Christian orphan in a Catholic boarding school in Namur. It took me a few months to get over my anger; it required all the indulgence, sympathy, and intelligence of Father André, the priest who was sheltering us, for me to finally realize that my sister had saved me from a tragic fate. When I admitted that, I was struck down with flu, and spent two weeks writhing on a bed in the infirmary with a temperature of 104.

But—and this is something I concealed from you—this situation didn't last until the end of the war.

In 1944, somebody gave me away and the Nazis took me.

It all happened in a rather strange way. The Germans had grown nervous since the Allied landings, and Father André, our protector, was becoming more and more fearful of being visited by them, so he faked our escape. As far as the school knew, we had run away one night in June 1944, but in reality we had taken refuge in the attic of the steward's lodge, where we had to move about quietly, speak in low voices, never put our heads out through the dormer window, and not smoke. Twice a day, Father André would bring us provisions and leave again with our dirty water. The entrance to the attic was hidden at the back of a closet: to get through, Father André had to take down the shelves. One Thursday, though, on the stroke of noon, we heard the sound of cars on the gravel of the courtyard. The Nazis headed straight for the closet, took out the contents, knocked down the door, and came upstairs to arrest us.

They hadn't hesitated. It was as if they had known where to find us.

I won't linger over what happened next. All my life, I've tried to blot out those months, tried to convince myself that I didn't live through them.

There was the journey by truck, the arrival at the Dossin barracks in Mechelen, the transit camp for the Jews. Already, there was the hunger, the lack of sleep, the confiscation of what little we owned, the blocked toilets, the moaning of the women, the cries of the children. And above all the waiting. The absurd waiting . . . we were waiting for the train we dreaded to arrive at any moment. We weren't living: as we expected the worst, we had stopped ourselves from living. It was the same thing I went through when your mother left us: the doctors had told me she only had a few hours left and I had decided to watch over her. She was unconscious, and breathing heavily. I don't know if you'll believe this, but at about three in the morning, exhausted, I dozed off and what woke me with a start was the silence! Yes, not the noise, but the silence, because it meant that Édith had drawn her last breath. A hundred times, every time her breath was late coming, I sat up on the extra bed, in a panic.

So, stupidly and obstinately, we waited in the transit camp. My classmates and I had already learned from the BBC what was happening to Jews sent to Poland. Many of those around us didn't know, while even more denied it. I kept silent—why add horror to fear?

Then the time came for my train.

Yes, I say "my train," because I had been waiting for it, preparing myself for it, my destiny was being fulfilled. Forced into a cattle truck by Flemish SS guards, the only thing I wondered was whether it was the same one that had taken Grandmother, Grandfather, Daddy, Mummy, and Rita away.

I wasn't afraid. Or else I was numb with fear. In fact, I no longer felt anything at all. An understanding deeper than my consciousness was protecting me from suffering by making me indifferent.

One train followed another.

One stop followed another.

We were dying of cold, thirsty, huddled together. Nothing belonged to us anymore, not time, not space.

German SS guards ordered us out.

Why here and not somewhere else?

On the platform, I discovered what my parents had lived through: the selection process, separation from the people you know. In a few minutes, I lost my classmates.

The group I was assigned to walked in the darkness to a hut, where we were piled in. Not finding a place free on the straw mattresses filthy with excrement and cockroaches, I crouched with my back to the wall and, sucking a splinter of wood to fool my appetite, dozed off.

I was fifteen.

I broke off reading, opened the window, and breathed in the country air, the scent of burned wood mingling with the pungent odor of decaying leaves.

Samuel Heymann was taking me to a place I didn't want to go. A place nobody would want to go . . .

Would I be capable of enduring the rest of his story?

Shaken, I found a few diversions for myself, sorted some books, folded three shirts, and convinced myself that I couldn't do without tea. Taking refuge in the kitchen, I became engrossed in contemplating the water as it simmered then boiled, then poured it, and watched attentively as the herbal teabag spread its brown tentacles through the teapot. Once the liquid had taken on the aroma of bergamot, I savored it as if drinking it for the first time.

Reassured by this ritual, I went back to what Samuel Heymann had written:

> In the morning, I woke up feeling different, with an indisposition that was going to prove tenacious in the days that followed: hope.
>
> The meaning of my previous patience was becoming clear . . .
>
> The only reason I had endured that harassment was because I wanted to see my family again. I didn't care what was done to me: being stripped naked, washed, deloused, my hair shaved, a number tattooed on my forearm, being forced to eat revolting food, working in the factory after exhausting marches. I never wavered, I looked everywhere, even in the most distant of the huts, certain that I would see my family.
>
> I questioned as many of the prisoners as I could. Whenever I approached, they saw how young and strong I was, and guessed what had happened to me, even what I was going to ask them. Some shook their heads long before I told them my parents' names. Those among us who had the luck not to be gassed became beasts of burden who barely lasted more than six months. It was unlikely that Mother, Father, Grandmother, Grandfather, or Rita had survived.
>
> Coming to this realization had an unexpected effect on me: I lifted my head and vowed that, whatever happened, I would resist. Yes, even if they were dead, whatever tortures

they had suffered, I would stay alive. It was an obligation. I owed them that. Rita had given me that destiny forever: to survive.

My sister had appointed me, I was the chosen one, I would never be a victim. Rita had taken risks for me. She may even have sacrificed herself for me . . . If I died, I would kill her a second time . . .

I tried therefore to apply that resolve.

Alas, I was living in a world where resolve had no place. The purpose of the camp was to turn us into animals, to break our individual wills. Whatever we had that was human, Auschwitz took it from us: when we arrived we had already lost our homes, our social standing, our money if we had any; if we stayed, we would lose our names, our clothes, our hair, our dignity, walk naked—naked even in our prison uniforms, another kind of nakedness—tattooed, reduced to numbers, ruthlessly exploited, tools to be used, bodies to be experimented on by the doctors. Like cattle, I was becoming an object in the hands of a superior race, the Nazis, who granted themselves the right to do whatever they liked with me.

At first, I had the foolish idea that I was having an adventure. I even remember taking refuge in a kind of ironic reserve, noting the stages of my degradation. A consciousness remained, that of a shy adolescent who believed in existence, who had decided to live, even through terrible ordeals.

But, with all the exhaustion and injustice and torture, all the pain, I was dwindling.

How to stop being humiliated and suffering from it? By telling yourself you don't deserve any other fate than the one you've been given; by agreeing to be what other people make of you; by considering yourself less than a pig, a piece of shit—in short, by abdicating your inner life. After five months, I no longer took refuge in my mind, I was nothing more than my cold skin, my cracked feet, my belly tight with hunger, my ass spewing endless diarrhea, my exhausted muscles that no longer responded to me. Sometimes, I even left my body, and became the cold, the hunger, the pain.

My survival plan had faded; only a primeval animal instinct, which depended on neither will nor morale, kept me alive. I crawled. I fought over a crust of bread. I obeyed the kapos to avoid being beaten. When one of us lay dying, it no longer affected me, I simply searched the body to make sure he wasn't hiding any food, or any object that could be swapped for something I wanted. During the marches to the factory and back, I stepped over corpses without compassion; my eyes remained dry and empty, like those of the dead; there was no time to weep. If I happened to recognize the face of a corpse, I envied it: here was a cold body that had stopped feeling the cold.

Because the dark, windy Polish autumn already had the icy edge of winter. One morning, I was shivering so much that, seeing the chimneys in the distance belching smoke, the origin of which I suspected, I imagined myself there, in the middle of the fire, fulfilled, dilated, radiant. Oh yes, I dreamed of burning in the oven to stop the shivering. Those fires on my body, caressing it. Flames of joy. My teeth have stopped chattering. What beneficial heat . . .

Once again, I laid Samuel Heymann's pages aside. I felt enormous guilt, guilt at reading this confession before Miranda had, guilt at having always talked with Samuel Heymann in total ignorance of the fact that he had been through an ordeal like that. How stupid and superficial I must have seemed to him!

I looked at the silver print that had been slipped in behind the letter, and recognized what it was: the photograph François Bastien had mentioned during our visit to the kennel. There, beside a barbed wire fence, stood a skeletal adolescent in a

strange uniform, in the company of a dog whose ribs stuck out
so much you could count them. The young man looked like
Samuel Heymann, or at least the way you might have imagined
Samuel Heymann as a starving adolescent; as for the
Beauceron, it was the exact double of the Argos I had known.
Already, you could see the master and the beast living in per-
fect harmony, both distracted by the camera but smiling at it.
Who was imitating whom? The dog, the master? The master,
the dog? When and where had this photograph been taken?

Decidedly, I had to read this text right through to the end.

*I'm coming now, Miranda, to the essential moment that
will allow you to understand the kind of father you lived with.*

*It was January 1945. We'd had no news of the fighting, we
didn't know if the Americans had made any progress since
the Normandy landings, if the Russians were advancing on us
or retreating, in short, we continued to trudge through the
snow, suffering through a winter that seemed endless.*

*I was aware of how weak I had become. I could see it in
myself and also in Peter, a Fleming who had arrived in
Auschwitz at the same time as me. This tall, well-built boy
with magnificent teeth had become an emaciated rat with
spindly feet, gray in complexion, his features hardened, dark
shadows under his eyes. He was like a mirror image of me.
What surprised me was that in the middle of his furrowed
face, he had kept his big, shiny, healthy teeth; I often looked
at them surreptitiously, clinging to those pieces of enamel like
a dying man to a buoy because I told myself that, when they
fell, we would all die.*

*The cold, the wind, the snow had taken root deep down
inside us. Although we still worked in the factory, we had the
impression that it required less of us, that the work was
becoming lighter; we refused, though, to think openly that
German industry was running at less than full capacity, for*

fear that the hope would poison us; to me it was a godsend, after the efforts I had been making to allay suspicion, to demonstrate that I was still healthy, useful, and efficient.

One morning, we were told we'd be staying in the camp that day.

Warning bells rang in what remained of our intelligence. Were we going to be executed?

After a day spent trembling with fear, the following dawn brought the same news: no factory today. We realized then that, with orders lessening, the factory was idle.

In spite of the cold, some of us got some fresh air.

I was walking along the sides of the huts when I saw three soldiers talking to a dog that was leaping about on the outside of the barbed wire fence. The men kept throwing snowballs at it, and each time the dog would chase after the ball, believing—or pretending to believe—that it was solid enough for him to catch it in his mouth. Obviously, each time, it would crumble in his jaws and he would bark in surprise, as if someone had played a bad trick on him. The three Germans would burst out laughing. From my hidden vantage point, I too was amused by the dog's stubbornness, his leaps and bounds, the carefree gaiety with which he ignored his failures and kept starting all over again.

Then the three soldiers heard a bell summoning them to resume their duties and walked away. When they disappeared from the animal's sight, the dog, unable to get through the fence, tilted his head to one side, whined with disappointment and sat down, looking bewildered.

I stepped forward. Why? I don't know . . . Especially since it was very unwise for a prisoner to wander too close to the edge of the camp. Never mind, I stepped forward.

As soon as he saw me, the dog wagged his tail and gave me a big smile. The closer I got, the greater his euphoria. He was stamping with impatience.

Without thinking, I grabbed some snow and threw a ball of it over the wire. Enthusiastically, he leaped up in the path of the projectile, seized it, reduced it to powder in his teeth, protested, then turned to me with a yelp, beaming with pleasure. I did it again, several times. He would rush at the ball, his hindquarters driven forward by some invisible, irrepressible force, abandoning himself to the intoxication of the race, swerving, tumbling, completely given over to his passion for movement.

I fell to the ground, my knees in the snow, my torso on my thighs, hot tears running down my cheeks. How good it was to cry at last . . . How long was it since I had last cried? How long was it since I had last felt anything? How long was it since I had last reacted like a human being?

When I looked up, the dog was sitting snugly in his rough fur coat, staring at me, questioning, anxious.

I smiled at him. He pricked up his ears, looking for a confirmation. His posture said, "Should I be worried or not?"

I was crying even more but insisted on smiling. For the dog, that wasn't a clear answer.

I walked toward him. He moaned with satisfaction.

When we were within a few feet of each other, he yapped shrilly and tried to push his muzzle between the barbed wire. Bending forward, I felt his warm breath on my palm, his damp, soft nose. He was kissing me. I started talking to him, I talked to him as I had never talked to anybody in the camp.

What did I tell him? That I was grateful to him. That he had made me laugh, which was something I hadn't done for a year. Above all, that he had made me cry, and that those tears were tears not of sadness but of joy. He had overwhelmed me by accepting me after the soldiers. Not only had I not thought he would give me such a warm welcome, I hadn't even thought he would see me. Most of the time I was transparent, nobody took any notice of me. According to the Nazis,

I belonged to an inferior race, good only for dying, or for working hard before dying. A race even below his, because the soldiers liked animals. When he had shown me how pleased he was to see me, I had become a man again. Yes, as soon as he had looked at me with the same interest and the same impatience as he had looked at the guards, he had given me back my humanity. In his eyes, I was as much a man as the Nazis were. That was why I was sobbing . . . I had forgotten I was a person, and I was no longer expecting to be shown any respect. He had restored my dignity.

Happy to discover my voice, he fixed his mahogany eyes on mine, his face grimacing, now with approval, now with disapproval. I was certain he could understand what I said.

Once I had calmed down, I noticed how thin he was. His ribs were visible through his skin, his bones protruded everywhere. He too was lacking in the necessities. And in spite of that, he was taking the time to amuse himself . . .

"You're hungry, aren't you, old boy? I'd really like to help, but I can't do a thing for you."

He drew in his tail even more between his hind legs. Although clearly disappointed, he wasn't angry with me. He continued to gaze at me with trusting eyes. He expected something wonderful, convinced I could perform miracles. He had faith in me.

Can you imagine it, Miranda? I had fought over stale bread, I had searched dead bodies looking for crumbs, but now, at lunchtime, I put a portion of beans in a cloth and took it to him that afternoon.

When he saw me, his tail lashed the air, and his back quivered. In all the hours he'd waited, he hadn't doubted me. His joy moved me all the more in that I wasn't going to disappoint him. I dropped the beans through the wire and he charged at them. In four seconds, my treasure had been devoured. He looked up: "More?" I told him that was all I had. He passed his tongue several times over his chops and seemed to accept my explanation.

I quickly ran away. Hearing him whine, I walked faster. When I reached our hut, my heart thumping, I told myself off: I had exposed myself to too many risks for a mutt, depriving myself of my own ration, walking too close to the fence. And yet, almost unwittingly, I began singing to myself. The other prisoners were startled.

"What's gotten into you?"

I started laughing. Certain that I had gone crazy, they turned away and went back to whatever they had been doing before.

The song was louder in my brain than what emerged through my cracked lips: I realized that the dog had brought me happiness.

Every day after that, taking advantage of the unusual idleness, I crept away to feed him.

A week later, the camp was liberated by the Russian army.

I confess that none of us had really believed it would happen. Of course, there had been some advance signs—soldiers leaving, squabbles among the kapos, noises in the night, cars coming and going—but, even when we saw our liberators with their red stars, we hesitated. Was it a trap? Some perverse trick dreamed up by the Nazis? Surprised or disgusted by our appearance, the Soviet infantrymen in their long coats stared at us in horror; we probably looked more like ghosts than human beings . . .

Nobody smiled at the soldiers, nobody thanked them. We didn't move, didn't speak—gratitude was a virtue we had long forgotten. It was only when the Russians opened the food stores and summoned us to the feast that we consented to make a move.

It was a ghastly scene. We fell on the pieces of ham, bread and meat paste like termites attacking a piece of wood, mechanically, heedless of whatever was around us. There was no pleasure in our eyes, only the fear of being interrupted.

Some died a few hours later from this abundance, because their bodies could no longer bear to ingest food. Who among them cared? At least they'd died with their bellies full.

At midnight, once I had eaten my fill, I said good night to Peter, the boy with the beautiful teeth, then walked along the fence looking for the dog . . . After the miracle that had just happened, I saw him as the herald angel, the bringer of glad tidings. His appearance on the scene had made it possible for me to bear the days preceding my liberation. In my pocket, I had kept for him a piece of meat paste I was looking forward to seeing him eat.

I didn't see him. I talked and sang in the hope that he would pick up my voice, but he never appeared.

I felt extremely sad. I burst into tears. It was absurd, of course, to cry on an evening like this when I had just come back to life, regained my freedom . . . I had merely clenched my jaws over the deaths of my parents, and yet I felt sorry for a stray dog I had only known for a week.

The next day, I was part of the group that left the camp.

Once more, we walked for hours across the white plain. Nothing had changed. We were back with the same forced marches we had already suffered . . . Some collapsed, just as had happened before. And just as had happened before, nobody stopped to prevent them dying in the powdery snow.

Suddenly, to the left of the column, I heard barking.

The dog was running toward me.

I kneeled and held out my arms. He threw himself against my chest and frantically licked my mouth. His tongue surprised me, disgusted me a little, scratched me a lot, but I let him cover me with slobber. This dog kissing me with such love was the girlfriend who wasn't waiting for me, the family I no longer had, the only creature who had looked for me.

The other prisoners overtook us, continuing on their way in the snow. The dog and I continued laughing and yelling, drunk with joy, happy to be reunited.

I didn't get up until the tail of the convoy was out of sight.

"Come on, dog, we have to stick with them or we'll be lost."

He nodded his flat head, grinning from ear to ear, his tongue lolling from right to left, and ran by my side to rejoin the group. Where did we get the strength?

At the end of that day, we spent our first night together. Subsequently, nothing ever separated us, not even a woman— I didn't meet your mother until he had left me.

In the school where our group stopped overnight, my animal huddled against my thighs, I suffered less from the cold than my companions. Better still, stroking his satiny skull, I rediscovered the contact, the tenderness, the weight of a physical presence. I was blissful. When was the last time I had willingly touched a warm body? For a moment, I had the feeling that my exile was over: wherever I was, as long as I had my dog beside me, I would be the center of the world.

At midnight, while the marchers were snoring and the moon hovered behind the misted-up windows, I looked hard at my sated companion, his ears pinned back against his head, his guard-dog stance relaxed, and gave him a name. "I'm going to call you Argos. That was the name of Odysseus's dog."

He frowned, not sure he understood.

"Argos . . . Do you remember Argos? The only living creature that recognized Odysseus when he returned to Ithaca in disguise after twenty years' absence."

Argos nodded, more to be obliging than because he was convinced. In the days that followed, he liked recognizing his name in my mouth, then proving to me, by obeying me, that it really was his.

Our return was slow, broken, and erratic. The strange

cohort of Auschwitz survivors staggered across a devastated, deprived Europe, where migrants joined grief-stricken local populations uncertain who their masters were. We, the skeletons, were dragged from temporary Red Cross posts to permanent ones, depending on what transport and lodging was available, trying to avoid the last of the fighting. To get back to Namur, I crossed Czechoslovakia, Romania, Bulgaria, before getting on a ship in Istanbul, sailing via Sicily, landing in Marseilles and traveling across France by train as far as Brussels. During that journey, Argos never left me. Of the people we met, some merely shrugged, but many remarked on how well trained he was ... Not that I had tamed him or forced him to do anything—I was too unfamiliar with the world of dogs— but united by affection as we were, we were delighted to hear this. I just had to think about turning left for Argos to veer in that direction. When I examine the photograph that an American soldier took of us in a makeshift camp, I realize that, in spite of the shortages, the discomfort, the uncertainty, the anxiety, we drew our energy from being together. The only thing we wanted from life was each other's company.

Even when he was starving, Argos waited while I chewed my bread. A man would have jumped me and grabbed it; he waited trustingly, certain that I would give him a piece. Yet I wouldn't have yielded my portion to anyone! His respect was making me a good person. If men are naïve enough to believe in God, dogs are naïve enough to believe in men. With Argos looking at me, I might become a human being again.

In the course of that odyssey, I barely thought about my relatives. Whereas so many of the survivors I met dreamed of rejoining their loved ones, assuming that if they themselves had pulled through, why not their fathers and mothers, I had given up on that aspiration. Deep down, an instinctive certainty told me that none of my family were still in this world.

When I got to Namur, I walked up the stairs to our apartment and knocked at the door.

Seeing again the waxed landing, the familiar sounds and smells, during the three seconds when I waited at the door with its peeling paint, my heart was pounding: I assumed that a miracle might happen. The totally banal sound of the lock moved me almost to tears.

A woman in a short nightdress looked out at me. "Can I help you?"

"I . . . "

"Yes?"

I leaned forward to peer at the two rooms behind the woman. Little had changed—not the wallpaper, the curtains, the furniture—only the inhabitants: a husband in a white singlet sitting facing a bottle, two little girls pushing a cardboard box across the floor.

Of course, the apartment had been rented out again . . . At that moment, I realized I had nothing left and that I was alone in the world.

"Er . . . I'm sorry, I must have the wrong floor."

I didn't dare tell her that I had lived there . . . I guess I was afraid the Gestapo would immediately show up.

She made a skeptical face.

On tiptoe to give credence to my mistake, I walked upstairs.

While I did so, this woman who had usurped my mother's place muttered as she closed the door, "He doesn't seem very bright, that one."

I knocked at the door upstairs. My neighbor opened, and took fright at first, her beautiful face tensing. She didn't dare trust her intuition. "Is it . . . you? Is it really you?"

"Yes, Madame Pasquier, it's me, Samuel Heymann."

She opened her arms, I threw myself into them, and we both wept. It was mysterious. While that embrace lasted, a *woman who was almost a stranger became my mother, my father, my grandparents, my sister, all those I missed, all those who, if they had lived, would have been so happy to know I had come back.*

In the weeks that followed, that good woman supported me as much as she could. She provided me with a small room at the top of the building, enrolled me in high school, made sure I ate and dressed decently. Then one Sunday—the most wonderful surprise of all—she took me to have lunch with Father André, my benefactor, who hugged me so tightly he almost choked me.

Father André and Madame Pasquier acted as my guardians. Argos was our only point of friction. Madame Pasquier and the father both considered it absurd to feed an animal at a time when it was hard enough to feed a human being. Bowing my head, I would reply that I didn't care, that I would always give half my portion to Argos, however tiny it was and even if it meant that I would die. Madame Pasquier would turn red when she heard that; generous as she was, there was still an order to things, and men came before dogs. But I didn't want to hear any more about a scale of values among living creatures; I had suffered too much from hierarchies; as a subhuman in a land of supermen, I had seen people like me die. Maybe I had even consented! So I didn't want to hear anything more about inferior or superior races! Never! Even though she sensed the bitterness in my words, Madame Pasquier reiterated her principles; in practice, however, whenever she saw us together, sensing that Argos was more than an animal to me, she did not insist.

Now that I was back in a normal situation, I started having normal thoughts: I was hungry for revenge, I wondered who had given away the ten Jewish children hidden by Father André. While continuing with my studies, I began an investigation.

I reflected, I revisited my memories with an inquisitorial eye, retrospectively analyzing the thoughts and attitudes of some of my classmates and finding out what had become of them. I don't have time, Miranda, to tell you all the leads I followed, including the false ones, that whole tangled web of suppositions that led me to suspect one boy rather than another, I'll simply tell you the conclusion I reached: a fellow pupil named Maxime de Sire had told the Gestapo where I was hiding.

Maxime de Sire was the same age as me, fifteen. He had rich parents and an exalted idea of himself, and he loved a challenge. God knows why, but in September 1943, he had decided that I would be his rival, that the school year would be a contest between him and me. What made the idea all the more preposterous was that, being gifted with more self-importance than talent, he consistently achieved poor grades. In everything—science, arts, Latin, Greek, even sports—he'd lean toward me and whisper, "You'll see, Heymann, I'll beat you hollow." I'd simply shrug my shoulders phlegmatically, which would make him even angrier. One day, I don't know how, he started to suspect that I was Jewish. At that point, everything changed: emulating me was no longer a spur to him, it was an expression of hatred. Even though my results were better than his, to him I embodied deception, I was the scandalous product of a cursed race that had no other purpose on earth than to tarnish, soil, pervert, and destroy. The anti-Semitism so common in his background gave him a key to understanding: no, he wasn't inferior to me at all, I was a monster descended from a hateful lineage. Several times, in catechism class, he spoke up to express his horror of "the Jewish race." However hard Father André tried to respond, refuting him point by point and invoking the name of Jesus, Maxime de Sire, with that impeccable middle part in his hair and his brand-new leather ankle boots, would sit down again, *pleased with himself, wink at his classmates, and retort to Father André that he respected him but that he also respected other intelligent men, like Charles Maurras, the intellectuals of Action française, Léon Degrelle, or the great Marshal Pétain who governed France.*

I think it was his behavior that led Father André, as a precaution, to fake our departure. When I questioned him about it after the war, he refused to answer. However, I have a clear memory that one morning, from the dormer window in the attic, I had seen Maxime de Sire standing in the middle of the mist-shrouded lawn, planted firmly on his legs, head raised, arms folded, looking up at the top floor with hostile eyes. Had he seen me? As I had withdrawn into the shadows, I can't be sure of that. In the days that followed—and this was a memory that took a while to come back to me—one or other of us claimed to have heard noises behind the door that hid our hiding place. Each time, he had thought it was Father André coming to pay us an unexpected visit. There was no doubt in my mind that Maxime de Sire had been verifying our presence before going to the authorities and revealing all.

I'm sure you'll tell me, Miranda, that you need more than that to accuse a man. But it was enough for me. I was convinced. In fact, I'm even more convinced now, you'll soon see why.

Having made inquiries about Maxime de Sire, I found out that he had just given up his studies to take care of his family's estate, which comprised several farms, some stables, and the trout pond concession.

One Sunday, I came to this region of the Hainaut. After all the miles we had walked across Europe on the way back from Auschwitz, my sedentary life had weighed heavily on Argos and he was pleased to rediscover the pleasures of a country stroll. Mixing pleasure and duty as usual, he thoroughly enjoyed his task of accompanying me. From time to time, I would take the stick I was using to walk with and throw it as far as possible into the grass; victoriously, he would bring it back to me like a trophy, always with the same energy, the same pride.

As luck would have it, when we had reached the Sires' château and I was walking alongside a hedge of alders, I caught sight, not far away to my right, of a horse trotting away, ridden by a familiar figure: Maxime was setting off for a ride in the woods.

I walked faster in his direction. Of course, I didn't think I'd be able to catch up with him, but I felt the need to pursue him.

In the middle of the various paths that crisscrossed the forest, I hesitated. I turned to Argos and asked him where the rider had gone. He sniffed the wind and, as if it were self-evident, started off in a southerly direction. We continued advancing.

After an hour, we were still walking . . . I finally had to admit I had lost my prey. It was then that the tall trees cleared, letting in a pool of bright green light; we came out to a pond strewn with duckweed. The horse had been tied to a lime tree. A hundred yards from there, I saw a crouching form: Maxime de Sire was picking mushrooms between the moss-covered stones.

I walked straight toward him, my stick in my hand.

He didn't see me coming. A twig cracked beneath my feet, surprising him, and he looked up. His eyes grew wide with fright. He had recognized me!

I charged straight at him, making no attempt to conceal my rage.

His mouth opened and let out a plaintive cry.

I accelerated. I had no idea what I was going to do, but felt an obscure necessity, stronger than me, behind every movement of my muscles. Was I intending to hit him? I don't think so. I wanted to confront him with his crime, but had no idea what form that would take.

When I was six feet from him, he rose to his full height and set off at a run. I realized that he had interpreted my sudden appearance as an attack and thought my stick was a weapon.

I found this reaction repulsive. What a wretch! Always thinking the worst! "Wait!" I cried. "Just wait!"

He was still running, letting out little piglike moans.

That was too much.

I set off after him.

Arms raised, clumsy and uncoordinated, his knees giving way, he was shrieking, "No, no."

In spite of my slowness, in spite of the year I'd spent in a concentration camp, I was running faster than him, especially as I was lighter. The idiot stumbled over a root and fell. Instead of getting up, he squealed like a stuck pig.

"Shut up, you imbecile," I hissed.

In response, he choked, he foamed at the mouth, he sweated, his eyes rolled upwards, he was soft, cowardly, despicable, already as prostrate as a sacrificial victim.

I decided to hit him. Since he was convinced that was my intention anyway, why deny myself? Breathing in, I released the violence that had been lurking deep in my brain, ready to pounce: yes, I was going to beat him to a pulp, I was going to take the law into my hands, into our hands, all of us, I'd leave him dead in a pool of blood. Revenge! He would pay for his crime. I'd avenge my parents, my grandparents, my sister, I'd avenge six million Jews by killing this babbling moron.

I raised my stick in the air . . .

It was then that Argos intervened: he charged at Maxime de Sire, placed his paws on his chest, and barked.

Maxime de Sire screamed, convinced that my dog was going to tear him to pieces. But Argos licked him once, then

broke free, yelped, and started running in circles around him,
enthusiastically, to let him know that he was ready to play.

I looked at Argos, disconcerted. What, hadn't my Argos,
who could sense my every mood, sensed my anger? Hadn't he
realized that I had to take the law into my own hands and get
rid of this scum?

No, the dog insisted, his head on the ground, his rump
high. He wanted to draw Maxime into an unforgettable
game. He barked impatiently. And that meant: "Come on,
we've wasted enough time, let's have some fun!"

Maxime stared at the animal, realized that he had nothing
more to fear from that direction, and looked at me again,
expectantly.

Argos threw me a wicked glance as if to say, "How slow
your friend is!"

Suddenly, I understood. Anger left my veins.

I smiled at Argos and threw the stick a long way.
Immediately focused, Argos ran to catch it before it touched
the ground. Maxime stared at me anxiously, pale-faced, lips
trembling.

I folded my arms across my chest. "Get up. The dog is
right."

"I beg your pardon?"

"The dog is right. He doesn't know you're a bastard, he
doesn't know you gave away my friends and me during the
war. As far as he's concerned, you're a man."

Argos put the stick down at my feet. I didn't react, too
occupied in looking Maxime up and down, so he scratched
impatiently at my shin.

"Of course. Go fetch, Argos!"

And to give him more credit, I sent the stick into the heart
of the undergrowth. This purebred dog who didn't know the
concept of race had just saved Maxime de Sire, just as he had
saved me a year earlier. It was impossible to explain that to

Maxime de Sire, because it would have meant telling an informer all about my private life.

Bursting with pride, Argos gave me back the stick with pieces of bramble still clinging to it. I signaled to him that we were turning back. Immediately in agreement, he fell into step with me, keeping the stick in his mouth, like a butler carrying his master's umbrella just in case it rains.

Muddy and disheveled, Maxime de Sire followed us at a cautious distance, calling after me to thank me, expressing himself with an unctuous humility as exaggerated as his arrogance had been:

"I don't have any excuse, Samuel. I behaved like a fool. I know that. We were confused. We were so dominated by the Nazis, we started thinking like them. I'm ashamed of my sin, I swear to you."

I listened without believing him. His contrition was too good to be true. All the same, deep down I was happy: I had tracked down the guilty party, I had confronted him with his actions, and Argos had rescued me for the second time. Without him, I would have behaved like a barbarian. After five years of war, he had helped me to rise above myself, by showing me what greatness is: a hero is a man who tries to be a man all his life, sometimes in opposition to others, sometimes in opposition to himself.

Well, Miranda, now you know my story. Our story, Argos's and mine. Your story too, since you knew the successive Argoses who have kept me going.

Without that dog, I would have been incapable of remaining in this world. Like so many survivors, I would have let discouragement overwhelm me, I would have kept repeating, "What's the point?", I would have sunk into depression and seized upon the first illness that allowed me to disappear.

Argos was my savior. Argos was my guardian. Argos was

my guide. He taught me everything: how to respect mankind, how to venerate happiness, how to live in the moment.

You can't admit these things in public: anyone claiming that a dog taught him wisdom would be thought of as insane. But that was what happened to me. Since that Argos died, the Argoses have taken over from one another, all similar and all different. I've always needed them much more than they needed me.

My last Argos was murdered five days ago. Five days is how long it's taken for me to write this confession. I say "my last Argos" because I don't have the time or the desire to travel to the Ardennes and find yet another puppy. First of all, I'm getting so old, I'll die before he will. Secondly, my last Argos reminded me so much of the original Argos that I loved him passionately, and I can't bear the thought that a dumb hit-and-run driver killed him. If I stay here, I'm going to start hating people again. And that's something I don't want: all the dogs I've had in my life have taught me the opposite.

To end, let me tell you an anecdote. Ten years ago, I met by chance, at an antiques fair, Peter, the boy with beautiful teeth I had known in the camp; he was now a patriarch with beautiful teeth. We retreated to a café to talk. He was a chemistry teacher, with an extensive family, and that day he was very angry because one of his grandsons had just announced to him that he was planning to become a rabbi.

"A rabbi! Can you imagine? A rabbi! Can we still trust God after what we've suffered? Do you believe in God?"

"I don't know."

"I don't believe in Him anymore and I'll never believe in Him again."

"I have to admit that when I was first in captivity, I prayed. For example, when we got off the train and the SS made their selection."

"Oh, yes? And do you think the others, the men, women and children who died in the gas chambers, didn't pray?"

"You're right," I said.

"Well, then, if God exists, where was He when we were dying in Auschwitz?"

Stroking Argos's head under our table, I didn't dare reply that God had come back to me in the eyes of a dog.

I lay there for a long time with Samuel's confession on my chest, reflecting on what I had just learned.

Outside, the clouds were racing, squat, light, rapid, like bowling balls on the blue lanes of the sky. The last leaves were falling from the trees and whirling between the smooth branches. As always in this very special region, the sun was shining with a warm golden light just before it set. The day had been gloomy, grey, and leaden, but now it was finding a way to make us miss it.

I realized that I had spent the whole day thinking about Samuel. It was time for me to take these pages to his daughter.

I wolfed down a sandwich and went to visit my dogs. Even though I had been away for several weeks and had only devoted a few minutes to them since my return, they gave themselves up to my caresses with abandon, and to my games with fervor, good-natured and idolatrous, never letting me forget that I was their master, even though Edwin, the caretaker, spent more time with them than I did. I usually called them "the most spoiled dogs in the world," but now, astonished by their lack of ingratitude, I suddenly doubted whether I deserved even a tenth of their devotion, and I made a fuss of them to console them for loving me.

I crossed the village to join Miranda.

She was idling in her father's garden, admiring the care with which he had reconstructed the quaint old gazebo and cut then arranged his firewood under the lean-to.

When she saw me outside the gate, she came running, sensing that something important had happened.

Anxiously, she unlocked the gate. I caught her by both hands and slowly, almost solemnly, placed the pages in them. She gave a start when she recognized her father's handwriting.

"What—"

"He wanted to tell you his secret before taking his leave. But because he didn't trust himself, he addressed it to me. He thought I ought to rewrite what he had written. He was wrong."

"But—"

"I'm going it read it out loud to you. That way, I'll have obeyed his wishes."

We sat down by the fire. I started a blaze, poured us two glasses of whiskey, and began the story. The text moved me even more the second time. Maybe because I was paying less attention to the events, and more to the way Samuel had written about them. Or was it because I could see how shaken Miranda was? Tears ran discreetly down her long, thin, pale face, but there was no sound of crying.

When I had finished, I poured us another glass. The silence was noisy with Samuel's reflections. Then we looked at each other, and went up to Miranda's room. There was only one thing to do: after that story of death and rebirth, which mixed the deepest despair with the wisdom of joy, we had to make love. We spent the night together, mischievous, respectful, alternating sensuality and sorrow, moving from laughter to astonishment, sometimes bestial, sometimes refined, always complicit. It was one of the strangest but most wonderful nights I've ever known.

*

The next morning, we went to the Café Pétrelle. We were

starving. The weather was so good that the owner had stuck a slate on the door: "Shady tables in the courtyard." We ate quickly because we had only an hour left to get dressed and go to Samuel's funeral.

The Count De Sire had not skimped on the pomp. An old hearse covered with wreaths of white roses appeared in the square, drawn by four quivering horses with gold harnesses, surmounted with ostrich plumes.

In the church, the profusion of flowers continued. A children's choir stood in the nave, with an orchestra lining the sides.

During the ceremony, three actors from the National Theater recited poems.

Maxime de Sire constantly threw nervous glances at Miranda to make sure she liked the proceedings.

"Look at him," she whispered in my ear. "He's still ashamed."

"All the better. That proves that he isn't just a villain. That he's trying to 'be a man,' as Samuel said."

"My father may have forgiven him, but he hasn't yet forgiven himself."

"That's something he can never do. Only the dead have the power to forgive."

MÉNAGE À TROIS

S he hadn't noticed him.

First of all, because he wasn't noticeable . . . He belonged to the mass of grey men who exhibit a front rather than a face, spineless characters who don't have bodies but merely a volume swelling their clothes, individuals we forget even if they pass us ten times, who come in and out without anyone paying attention to them, with less presence than a door.

So she hadn't noticed him.

To be honest, she'd stopped looking at men . . . She really wasn't in the mood. The only reason she still went out into society was to look for money. She needed it urgently! How was she to support her two children, to give them food and a roof over their heads? Her family had made it quite clear they wouldn't help her out beyond the summer. As for her sister-in-law, that tight-fisted bitch, there was no chance of help from that direction.

Yes, she had taken her time noticing him. Would she have picked him out at all from the others if he hadn't imposed his presence on her? If he hadn't shouldered his way toward her through the overpopulated drawing room?

Standing flat against the wall next to her, between the fireplace and a monumental bouquet, he had obliged her to look at him and then started up a conversation. It would be more accurate to describe it as a monologue, because she hadn't replied and had spent her time searching with her eyes for a man who might be useful to her among all the guests at this wretched party. Useful, in the sense of being a possible employer. She had to work hard, that was all she could do . . . As for men, it was all over for her! She had given enough. Or rather—and let there be no misunderstanding about this—she had given enough of herself to one man. Well, almost . . . Her husband. And he had just died. What had he been thinking of? He hadn't been much older than thirty . . . That was no age to die. Especially as he'd always been healthier than her. Whereas she had been forced to take frequent cures in Baden, he had never stopped moving, working, running around. Would she have married him nine years earlier if she had known that he would leave her alone without a penny, saddled with a thousand debts and two orphans? Of course not. Her mother had been against it! Good old Mother. But there you are, when you're twenty you don't know. Or thirty or sixty for that matter . . . We don't know the future because we make it.

The ectoplasm was still muttering away beside her. Just as well. This way, she didn't look abandoned. In this glittering society, there was nothing more humiliating than to seem like a loner: if you weren't one already, you soon became one. Vienna could be cruel to those who didn't play her game.

What was he saying? What did it matter? He was neither cold nor aggressive, which at least was something. He was like lukewarm water.

Look! What if she collared that eminent crow over there with his hooked nose and black silk suit? It was said that he organized concerts—and even paid the musicians well.

Yes, she ought to grab him.

Too late. He was gone . . .

It was then that her companion in boredom, the colorless fellow beside her, uttered her name.

"Do you know me?" she said in surprise.

He bowed and expressed his condolences.

"Have we met before?" she exclaimed.

"Your sister, that wonderful singer I had the opportunity to hear in Regensburg, told me of your tragedy earlier. Once again, my condolences."

What a silly fool I've been! she thought. *I've been looking for my prey at the other end of the room when he might be standing right next to me. Who is he? And where does that slight accent come from?*

Throwing herself eagerly into the conversation, she learned that he was a diplomat, recently arrived from Copenhagen, and that he had grown very fond of Vienna.

"Do you like music?"

"Passionately."

She didn't believe him. From having sized him up, she was sure he wasn't passionate about anything. He was trying to pick her up . . .

Amused, she decided to blow her own trumpet. "I sing," she said. "Oh, not as well as my sister, but not badly at all. Some people say I'm more moving."

"Is that so?"

"We both had the same teachers. The best there were."

He pursed his lips in admiration. She had hooked him. She was already thinking of her fee.

"Would you like me to come and sing for Denmark?"

He took her hand. "I'm not sure about Denmark. But I'd definitely like you to sing for me."

*

Was it possible she was still attractive?

She stared at herself in the mirror, trying not to linger over her faults. If you omitted the roll of fat on her belly—a legacy of her pregnancies—if you didn't mind broad hips and small breasts, if you were susceptible to tiny, oblong faces, if you called bulging brown eyes "big dark lakes," if you disregarded the fine lines on her eyelids, she wasn't too bad-looking.

That was a lot of *if*s, wasn't it?

And yet this man, who was no different than any other man—quite the contrary, in fact—was ecstatic over her.

She looked again at her reflection in the mirror. Since he thought of her as a beauty, she tried to see herself through his eyes.

This was so unhoped for! A young widow was already an old woman, but on top of that, a penniless widow with two children to support—well, nobody wanted any part of that! And yet this afternoon he was going to ask her to marry him. She was sure of it.

Maybe she'd soon be able to stop living from hand to mouth. She'd leave this grim one-bedroom apartment she was renting for almost nothing—although it was still too expensive—and move somewhere more suitable.

There was a knock at the door. Was it he? He hadn't been able to wait . . . He had come to pick her up! Luckily, the boys were having lunch at their grandmother's today . . .

She opened the door, but before she had had time to react, the bailiff had stuck his foot between the wall and the door. She held tight to the door handle.

"You're making a mistake, sir!"

"I'm not making any mistake. I recognized you. You can move as much as you like, but I'm on your trail. Pay me."

"You're harassing a woman who can't even feed her own children!"

"You owe me mortgage installments."

"My husband owed you, not me."

"You agreed to the inheritance."

"I never agreed to starve my children to make rich men fat."

"Money! Not words! Money!"

Unruffled, sure of his own strength, the bailiff kept pushing. He was going to get in . . . Seizing the wrought-iron hat stand just within her reach, she brought it down on his leather shoe.

The man screamed and instinctively pulled his foot away. She slammed and bolted the door. "You're not getting out of this so easily!" came his indignant voice. "I'll be back."

She sighed, relieved that he preferred to come back rather than wait. Otherwise how would she have been able to keep her appointment?

Annoyed at having been reminded of her precarious situation at the very moment she had been dreaming of better prospects, she sat down at her dressing table and untangled and smoothed her long black hair, an activity that always alleviated her worst anxieties.

An hour later, she joined her admirer in his bachelor apartment on Singerstrasse, which was in a very respectable neighborhood. A table laden with tea things and dozens of cakes welcomed her.

He wasn't rich, but neither was he short of money. He might not have been handsome, but he wasn't repulsive. He looked more like a coarse peasant in his Sunday best than a sophisticated diplomat, but he couldn't take his eyes off her.

"I have something to tell you," he said in a low voice.

She blushed, delighted that he wasn't wasting any time. Lowering her eyelids, holding her breath, and folding her hands over her right knee, she prepared herself to receive his proposal of marriage.

"I've been in a confused mood lately," he began, gravely.

She almost replied, "So have I," but refrained, not wishing to spoil this solemn moment.

"The thing is . . . How to put this? I . . . "

"Say it." She smiled at him encouragingly.

He blinked, overawed by the words he was about to utter. "It's . . . it's . . . about your late husband."

She stiffened. "I beg your pardon?"

"We've never talked about him," he went on.

"What's there to say, for heaven's sake?"

She immediately regretted this exclamation. What a trap! If she sneered at her late husband, she would appear an ungrateful woman, incapable of respect or affection. If, on the other hand, she spoke too lovingly of him, she would seem unready to embark on a new relationship. She had to wipe out the past, but do so in an elegant way.

"I was very young when I married him. He was amusing, generous, different, and he was mad about me. You're wondering: Did I love him?"

"Go on."

She risked her all and stated firmly, "Yes. I loved him."

His face relaxed.

What a relief! She had played the right card. "I loved him," she repeated. "He was my first love and my only love. One way or another, I'll always love him."

He made a face, and she panicked. By depicting herself in such a virtuous light, she realized, she was pushing him away. She had to keep the door open at all costs.

"I loved him all the more because I didn't see his faults. At the time, I thought he was brilliant, talented, with a great future ahead of him. He wrote music, you know . . . "

He heaved a sigh of approval.

She smiled. "Yes, you're right to mock. Composing music isn't a serious profession, not one that leads anywhere. Our society doesn't respect artists. Especially not artists who don't succeed."

"Society is wrong," he said.

She stopped for a moment. *Don't forget he loves music.*

"Anyway," she went on, in a more conciliatory tone, "he

wasted his time running after commissions and giving lessons when he should have been paying the rent. At first I put up with that chaotic life because I thought it was temporary. But after a few years . . . "

Here she felt like crying out, " . . . after a few years, I realized that he was a failure, that our life was falling into a rut, and that things would never get any better!" But out of consideration for her interlocutor's tastes, she toned down the anger she felt inside.

" . . . after a few years I realized he was too proud to be a success in his career. He wasn't a schemer. He wouldn't compromise. When it came to music, he considered himself superior. Superior to anybody else. And he had no qualms about saying it! As if it were self-evident. It was absurd . . . Obviously, he put off the very people who wanted to help him."

He stood up and circled the table, relieved.

That's it! she thought. *We've cleared the air. He's calmer now. At last he's going to declare himself.*

"I . . . "

How shy he is!

"I . . . "

"Are you afraid of me?"

He shook his head.

"I'm listening," she said in his ear.

"I . . . I liked the piece you sang the day before yesterday."

Music again? She hid her exasperation and replied in the kindest possible tone, "It was by him."

He went red with enthusiasm. "I was sure of it! I'd recognize his style anywhere."

She laughed inside. *His style? What style? He didn't have one, he imitated all the styles he came across. That's like saying blotting paper has a style!*

This conversation, which hadn't gone as expected, was starting to get her down. The man had something else in mind other than marriage: he wouldn't declare himself either today or tomorrow. How could she have been such a fool as to imagine he would? It must be down to the change of life . . . She had wanted to believe that she was still young, beautiful, desirable, all the things silly women still hope once they're past thirty. What an idiot! And anyway he was starting to bore her, this Dane. Maybe she should leave?

"Do you mind if I go now? I haven't been feeling well since this morning."

"Oh, what a pity, I've taken quite a fancy to you, and I was about to suggest that we live together."

*

All right, so he hadn't married her, but it was "as good as." They shared a comfortable apartment on Judenstrasse—rent paid by him—they ate together, slept together, and took care of the two boys—their education consisting essentially of sending them to a boarding school, which suited her to a T.

Did she have any reason to complain?

"What are you doing?" she shouted. "Are you coming?"

From the corridor, he replied with an indistinct murmur.

She shuffled the playing cards impatiently. She liked her Dane. Yes, he had lots of merits, and she appreciated them. Not any particular one, but all of them together. An anthology of merits. A volume of virtues. That set her mind at rest. His predecessor had displayed more faults than merits. Or rather, he'd had huge faults and intense merits. A rose covered in thorns. And what was this one? A big peony . . . No smell and merely a fleeting beauty . . .

She laughed. Poor man! She was always making fun of him. But not out of cruelty, out of affection. He was so industrious, so serious, so accomplished, so respectful, you just had to laugh, otherwise . . .

She stopped.

Otherwise what?

Behave, she told herself. *Don't spoil what you have.*

With the previous one, she hadn't needed to appear perfect, because he wasn't. With this one, she had to watch her step, restrain herself, hide from him the fact that she could behave like a nuisance, a strumpet, even a bitch—he wouldn't have understood, he wouldn't have found it funny. For the sake of this Dane, she had drawn a veil over whole areas of her personality. A widow's veil?

She chuckled.

He approached and kissed her hand. "Why are you laughing?"

"I don't know. Maybe because I'm happy."

"I love your mischievous temperament," he sighed.

"What was keeping you so long? Diplomatic dispatches?"

She hadn't the faintest idea what a diplomatic dispatch was but she had grown excessively fond of the term.

"No, I was sorting through scores."

"I'm sorry?"

"I was listing and dating your husband's scores."

She scowled. *What! Not again* . . . He was devoting all this time to the man she'd had such a difficult life with.

"My dear, you seem upset."

She put on a sulky expression. "For our sakes, I've forgotten the past. Whereas you keep reminding me about my husband."

"I'm not interested in your husband, but in the composer. He was a genius!"

Not that! Now he's as mad as the first one was! He was always praising himself to the skies! Why's this one doing the same?

"I'm jealous."

"What?"

"Yes, I'm jealous that you devote so much time to him, even though you're so overworked."

"Oh, come now, how can you be jealous of my relationship with your first husband? He's dead, and I never even knew him!"

"Why do you say 'first' husband? Do I have a second one?"

She looked at him witheringly, awaiting a response. He bowed his head, shamefaced, but said nothing.

In tears, she ran and shut herself in her room.

*

"You seem carefree," cried her sister.

"Oh, I am. Do you realize that before him I was living on charity? My composer left me with nothing but debts. He never held on to a job long enough for me to be entitled to a widow's pension! Incredible, isn't it? Not a penny."

"Well, when you think of the kind of man he was . . . "

"Now, thanks to my Dane, I manage to make a bit of money here and there. And he doesn't care how I use it."

Her Dane, as she called him, had found a way to earn her some money. After gathering together all the scores and making an inventory of them, he had set about trying to sell them. Amazing! When she thought that the manuscripts used to be lying about all over the place, under the piano, in the bed, in the kitchen, behind the cushions on the armchairs . . . But her Dane had gotten it into his head that they might be valuable, and he kept pestering publishers about them. The most surprising thing was that from time to time he succeeded! Right now, he even had two of them competing with each other. He was turning out to be a really good merchant, this *chargé d'affaires* at the Danish legation. And he was able to use legal language in such a way as to deliver rock-solid contracts. Besides, he was the one who carried out negotiations by appropriating her identity—she had unhesitatingly allowed him to use her signature. Sometimes, when she read over his shoulder the letters he was writing, she would double over with laughter seeing him mention his "dear dead husband."

Her sister nodded admiringly then added, "What about the rest?"

"He's very gentle, very steady, very considerate."

Obviously, he was nothing like the previous one. She was living with a gentleman now, who didn't swear, didn't spit, didn't belch, didn't fart, who spoke four languages but never used a vulgar word, and who asked her politely if they could make love. Had she ever seen him undressed? Not at all. She found this behavior "restful" and better suited to her age. All the same, she sometimes thought nostalgically of the crazy things the other one used to say, his unbridled sexuality, the many pleasures, including the most disreputable, into which he had initiated her . . .

"Do you love him?" her elder sister insisted.

"Of course!" she said, outraged. "What do you take me for?"

"So why doesn't he marry you?"

Irritated that her sister kept on asking her the very question she was constantly asking herself, she replied in a tone of assumed impassivity, "It's perfectly simple. When you work for the foreign service, it's best to stay single. If you burden yourself with a wife, you aren't considered flexible, and no longer get offered the best positions."

"Is that so?"

"Yes!"

"In Austria, though, we . . . "

"He's Danish."

"Of course . . . "

What she wouldn't admit, even though she had guessed, was that a diplomat only married if his wife's position added luster to his career. She didn't come from a respected family, she didn't bear a noble name, she was nothing but the widow of an obscure scribbler of music who'd always been one step ahead of the bailiffs . . .

"Who was it who told me that Danes were very good lovers?" her elder sister murmured languidly, rubbing her silky lips with her index finger.

Yes, who? she thought.

*

Now even the most malicious of scandalmongers were forced to admit that her life was a success.

The sun bounced off her diamond ring in a flash of light that was like a flash of laughter. He had married her! It had taken twelve years but he had married her!

In the distance, the ducks strutted on the lake between the weeping willows, as if they owned the grounds.

She had remained on the terrace to savor her happiness—she would join the guests later.

Baroness! Who would ever have though that she would become a baroness? At the age of forty-seven! After years of hardship, she had hit the jackpot. Everything had been against her: her age, a previous marriage, two sons, precarious health, a terrible financial situation, and the unfair reputation of being a scatterbrain incapable of running a household. And now the servants all bowed down to her! What's more, their wedding had been celebrated with a sumptuous ceremony in the cathedral in Pressburg, even though he was a Protestant and she a Catholic. She knew, of course, how pleased her sister had been for her, what she loved most was to think about her enemies, those vixens who thought she was finished . . . Oh, the anger of those stuck-up bitches when they learned of her marriage!

And her *Von*! She didn't just have a wedding ring, she also had a *Von*. Of course, her Dane made fun of her when she had herself called baroness and put a *Von* in front of their surname, constantly telling her that although he had recently been knighted by the state, it was merely an honorary distinction, and did not mean that the family had been ennobled.

"Nonsense! They knighted you, which means I'm a lady, and nobody will prevent me from adding the *Von* you lacked before."

Sometimes she would have liked to meet new people, just to show off her success. An audience . . . That was what was lacking here. Copenhagen was a pretty town, with its cute red houses, and she liked it a lot, but it wasn't Vienna! Calm, smiling men lived in slow motion here, occupied in guzzling beer or curdled milk.

Don't complain, she told herself, *and please don't bite the hand that feeds you.*

It wasn't boredom that she felt, more a kind of soft languor she couldn't shrug off. Was it because she had stopped dosing herself with coffee, the last bad habit that remained from her previous life? With that Bohemian pipsqueak she'd been married to, anything could happen at any time, for better or worse, but something always happened. Here the days were all the same, pleasant but identical. Walking, reading, tarot cards. It wasn't exciting, it was frankly dull, but if that was the price to pay for wealth, nobility, security . . .

She sighed and joined the guests, who were chatting in the drawing room.

"An outstanding composer, a truly outstanding composer!" her husband was saying in the middle of a group of men.

Again? It's becoming unbearable. Not only does he force me to talk about him when we wake up in the morning, but he's still holding forth about him in the afternoon. We're a threesome. Wherever I go, I have two husbands with me: the first, who's always being talked about by the second, and the second, who's always talking about the first.

He kept waving his hands and insisting, "It's about time Copenhagen discovered him. His works should be played here."

Poor man! He's trying to persuade people to buy my scores. It's kind of him, and when it works it brings in a few pennies. I suppose he works himself into the ground like this for me rather than for himself, but he doesn't need to, not now that he's been promoted and is earning four times as much as he used to.

"When we hear his music," he continued before his captive audience, "we realize that the man was a kind of angel."

What's he talking about? I've never met anyone coarser or more vulgar. An angel? An angel who never thought about anything but fornicating!

"Yes," he was saying, "it's clear he was inspired by God. Maybe he had an ear that directly seized what the Creator whispered to him."

What an idiot! My first husband used the same seven notes to depict Jesus Christ, a sinner, a young girl in love, or an adulterous wife. It was nothing but technique. Musicians' tricks.

"I had the misfortune to scribble terrible poetry in my youth before I gave it up, and I can recognize genius, believe me. Ladies and gentlemen, that man was a sublime composer."

You dummy! Stop talking about him, you're making a fool of yourself. He may have been a decent enough composer, but my God, how he fucked!

And, with a hiccup that everyone took to be a sign of the emotion caused by talk of her dead husband, she went back out onto the terrace.

*

Sitting back on the leather chair, with her legs apart, she

had been brooding for half an hour in front of this desk, her temples on fire, trying to avoid facing the facts, even though the evidence was right here before her eyes.

No doubt about it. Her second husband was writing the life story of her first husband.

A biography . . . That explained his unremitting activity over the past few years, that was why he cluttered their house with piles of newspapers, magazines, and programs, that was why he corresponded with those who had known the composer, even with her dragon of a sister-in-law, although she had expressly forbidden him to do so. Perhaps that was why he was so fond of talking with her about the past. What a betrayal! While she had believed he had simply been affectionately curious about his beloved's youth, he had actually been using her to gather information for his book.

Her first husband . . . always her first husband . . . He took up more space dead than he had when he was alive.

Overcome, she looked at the handwritten pages, determined to destroy them immediately. *What perversion is this? Why's he spending his time reconstructing my life with another man?* She picked up a page at random.

"His marriage was a happy one. His wife was a gentle, sensitive woman who loved and understood him. She admired him for the great artist that he was and was able to adapt to his character, which allowed her to gain his trust to such an extent that he loved her and told her everything, even his smallest faults. She rewarded him with her tenderness and her constant care and attention. She admits it even today: how could she not forgive him and be his entirely when he was such a good man?"

In spite of her bad mood, she smiled. What an innocent! He was telling the story just as she had told it to him. He had swallowed her lies. During their conversations, unshackled by the truth, she had depicted her conduct as it might have been rather than as it had been, enjoying giving herself a better role. For years now, she had been describing herself as her current husband would have liked her to act toward the previous one. More than anything else, she had done it to please the one who was alive, to justify and even inspire his love. She had been revisiting her first marriage through her husband's eyes in order to satisfy him.

Going through the following paragraphs, she received confirmation that he was drawing a wonderful portrait of her.

At least that'll make up for the treachery of my horrible sister-in-law!

With this exclamation, she found herself accepting this unusual project. To be honest, this biography served her purpose . . . Strangely—thanks to her Dane's campaigning—the dead man was being increasingly talked about, his works were being played, some composers claimed to be followers of his, even if only her sons' teachers! How bizarre fashion could be . . . Not that they should have any illusions: it wouldn't last. His music was old-fashioned, people were interested in something more modern. You couldn't change them. In spite of this brief revival, it would all soon be forgotten.

Anyway, if by some miracle people did take an interest in her, at least this biography didn't repeat the nonsense her in-laws had spouted about her.

A shadowy figure came up behind her.

"Are you looking through my things?"

She stood up and kissed him. "My dear, what you're planning is wonderful."

"Oh, yes?" he asked, dubiously.

"You know, he would have been proud of you."

Instead of replying, he turned red, his neck swelled with pleasure, and his eyes misted over.

He would have been proud of you. Looking at him, she realized that these words had plunged him into a more emotional state than the day he had been knighted. Or the day of their wedding.

*

"Yes, Mother, I assure you . . . "

"No, impossible, it's too ridiculous!"

"I swear to you. He asked me to talk to my aunt about it."

"Your aunt? Do you still see that bitch?"

"Mother, everyone knows she loves me . . . "

"All she sees in you is her brother's son, she forgets you're also mine. She's always hated me."

"Mother . . . "

"Never mind! That's not the question. You're saying that . . . "

"Yes, Stepfather told me he wanted to be buried with you in Father's vault . . . "

"What a nightmare!"

Exasperated, livid with anger, hair disheveled, she went straight to the library, which her husband used as an office, determined to break the polite silence with which she had accepted his eccentricities until now. Her second husband was so wild about the first, she had often had the feeling she was in a *ménage à trois*, but this was going too far . . . In a vault, the dead man would no longer be just a memory but would become a body again. All three of them, she and her two husbands, were going to find themselves lying for all eternity in the same room.

When she entered the library, he lay gasping for breath on the Persian carpet.

"Oh . . . my dear . . . you're just in time . . . "

He had had another dizzy spell—they had been occurring with increasing frequency for some time now. No wonder he was obsessed with death and tombs.

As she approached him, his face lit up. Poor man! How he loved her . . . His dull eyes shone with joy at the sight of his wife.

She immediately stopped nursing her anger and thought only of helping him, supporting his head, fanning him, cooling him down, letting him get his breath back.

This business of the tomb didn't really matter. She would talk about it later, when the moment was right.

She sat him down on the couch, surrounded by cushions. He was calmer now, and the color was coming back into his face.

"You scared me," she scolded him tenderly.

"There's life in the old dog yet."

I hope he's right! I don't want to be a widow again.

They held hands for a long time, gazing out at the coppery light of dusk. Then he turned to her, and with a solemn look on his face, said, "There's something I wanted to suggest, something that means a lot to me."

Oh no! He's going to bore my head off with that shared mausoleum and, given the state he's in, I won't be able to refuse him.

"Yes, my dear?" she replied in a steady voice.

"Use his name."

"I'm sorry?"

"Start using your former husband's name again."

Tears welled in her eyes. She felt as if she was going to choke. "What? Are you rejecting me?"

"No, my darling, I care for you more than ever. I'd simply like it if in society, as a mark of both his genius and my love, you called yourself Constanza Von Nissen, the widow Mozart."

A HEART UNDER ASH

Y ou know, Auntie, you don't have to lose every game . . ."
Gathering his aces and jacks, the boy in the cherry-red
T-shirt gave his aunt a gentle look. She quivered with
an indignation that was half-feigned, half-genuine.

"I'm not doing it on purpose. Either I'm bad, or you're
really good."

Jonas smiled, unconvinced, and started to shuffle the cards
again.

Alba gazed at the teenager—his frail chest, his long arms,
his tapering fingers—sitting cross-legged on the virgin wool
rug: even though he played regularly, he didn't have the dex-
terity of those who are used to cards; he wasn't fast, wasn't precise, wasn't fond of those broad gestures that impress the girls;
he handled the cards with composure.

She liked that about him. He never fell into the traps set for
young people. With nonchalant grace, he avoided the usual
effects, the vulgar desire to impress. He remained different.
Even if he had been raised by the worst of crooks, he wouldn't
have learned any bad ways.

She burst out laughing. "I wonder if either of us really likes
this game."

Intrigued, Jonas looked up again, making his head of blond
hair shake.

"What if we discovered one day," she went on, "that neither
of us could stand old maid, Russian bank, or belote, but that
we were pretending, just to keep each other happy?"

He laughed, then sighed. "Well, anything I did just to please you would please me, too."

His words moved her. How handsome he was, with his well-defined lips, as red as his sweater . . .

"Me too," Alba murmured, fighting her emotions.

Why weren't men like him? Pure, simple, attentive, generous, easy to love? Why did she get along better with her nephew—who was also her godson—than she did with her son or her husband? She shook her head to dismiss these thoughts and cried, "You're a sorcerer!"

"Me?"

"Or a magician."

"Oh, yes? What tricks can I do?"

"Steal hearts," she said, leaning forward and pinching his nose.

As she did so, she had the fleeting, unpleasant impression that she hadn't found the right tone, doubtless because she was forcing her smile or exaggerating her cheerfulness.

Jonas's eyes clouded over, and his face changed. Shifting his gaze to the window, he murmured, a bitter crease at the corner of his mouth, "Sometimes, I'd like to do that."

She shuddered. What a fool she had been! She had just realized the incredible stupidity of her words. Steal hearts! The very words to avoid with a boy who . . .

She stood up, her temples throbbing, wanting nothing more than to run away. *Quick, create a diversion! Wipe out the gaffe. Don't let him think about his misfortunes . . .*

She ran to the window. "I'm bored with cards! What would you say to a walk?"

He stared at her in surprise. "In the snow?"

"Yes."

She was delighted at his surprise. In suggesting going out, she wasn't treating him like his cautious mother, who always kept him in the warm bosom of the house.

"Auntie, we're going to slip."

"I hope so!"

"Hooray! I'm your man."

As feverish as dogs being taken for a walk, Alba and Jonas looked through the closet in search of the appropriate gear, and, as soon as they had put on parkas, thick gloves, and fur-lined boots, they ran outside.

The cold greeted them, sharp and bracing, living up to their expectations.

Arm in arm, they advanced along the path.

It was a dazzling morning. The sun shone out of a clear blue sky. Around them, the snow had erased rocks, ponds, roads, and meadows; all was whiteness, from the cliffs to the hills, a whiteness in which a few houses were nestled, a whiteness interspersed here and there with copses of dwarf birches, a whiteness crisscrossed with streams like black stripes.

From below, the sea cast its breath up to them, a powerful smell of salt and seaweed, a smell that fed on the vastness.

Jonas quivered. "Do you think we're at the beginning of spring or the end of winter?"

"March 21 is only the middle of winter. The sun's higher but not the barometer. There are still frosts and snowfalls."

"I'm crazy about my country!" Jonas cried.

Alba smiled. What point of comparison did he have, this boy who had never yet left his island? His enthusiasm expressed something else: the fact that he cherished life, that he enjoyed existing, even if, like the local climate, he went though some rough moments.

A cell phone rang. Jonas took a while to answer because of his gloves. It was his friend Ragnar.

Listening to him, he turned pale.

"What is it?" Alba asked anxiously.

"Eyjafjöll has erupted."

"What? The volcano?"

"Last night . . . "

Jonas resumed his conversation with Ragnar, listening to what the latter had to tell him. At that instant, Alba panicked. The "cabin"! The little house where she and her sister had spent their childhood was near Eyjafjöll. Had it been touched by the seismic shocks? By the jets of lava? By the showers of ash?

As Jonas watched her, she walked around in circles, crunching the hard snow, tormented by anxiety. For two centuries, the volcano had been dormant, and during that long sleep, generations of her family had lived in that wooden cabin with its roof of earth and grass . . . Of course, even in her mother's day, and then for her sister and her, the cabin had been just a holiday home, where they spent thirty days a year, far from the city, but those days were wonderful, filled with a sense of their past, the centuries-long history of the Ólafsdóttirs.

Jonas hung up and hastened to inform his aunt. "They've declared a state of emergency. There was an eruption at the Fimmvörðuháls pass. They're going to evacuate the inhabitants of the village of Fljótshlíð for fear of floods."

"Floods?"

"Because of the heat of the lava, the compacted snow and blocks of ice will turn to water, Auntie."

She could breathe more easily: the cabin wasn't anywhere near there!

In thinking that, she realized she hadn't spared a second's thought for the farmers. Because the house remained empty all through the year, she had stupidly generalized from her own case, neglecting the fact that other Icelanders who lived in the area would have their livelihoods endangered.

"Do they have any idea what's going to happen next?" she asked.

"The geologists say it may last a while."

"I'm going there tomorrow."

Energetically, she took Jonas's arm again, as if they were setting out on a journey.

For a few yards, the boy proceeded at her pace, then she sensed that his breathing had turned to panting and that he was holding her back.

She turned: Jonas's face was drained of color, his lips were pursed, and he was breathing grey steam into the air.

"Are you all right, Jonas?"

"You're too quick for me."

He can't manage even as much as he used to, she thought, *it's getting worse. Did I do something stupid by suggesting we go out? Katrin's right to keep him indoors. Let's go back quickly. Well, no, not quickly—as calmly as possible.*

She had the impression that Jonas had heard her, because he calmed down and gripped her elbow. They walked back cautiously, with measured steps.

Once inside, Alba suggested hot chocolate. Over two steaming cups, sitting in the brushed steel kitchen, they resumed their chat.

"I shouldn't say this out loud," Jonas declared, "but I love natural disasters."

"Are you crazy?"

"I love the fact that nature's strong, that it humiliates us, that it reminds us of its power, that it puts us in our place."

"Then welcome: Iceland is the country where you should have been born."

"Do you think we choose, Auntie? Do you think our soul flies over the world, looks down, and then decides, 'Oh, look, I'm going down there, to that piece of land, to that family, because they suit me'?"

"Some say so."

"I'm sure of it. I got together with the angel who was taking care of me and we both thought that Mother and you were the only people capable of dealing with a burden like me."

Alba blushed. She didn't know if she loved or hated what her nephew had just said, but it moved her deeply. In fact, Jonas had been disconcerting her ever since he had appeared, ever since, in the maternity ward, she had received him from the arms of an exhausted Katrin and he had looked up at her. From his first minute of life, the boy had decided that he would have two mothers, the Ólafsdóttir sisters. And neither had objected. Strangers were sometimes surprised that such a close bond should exist between nephew and aunt, godson and godmother, but as far as the three of them—Jonas, Katrin, and Alba—were concerned, this attachment was perfectly natural. When, eight months later, Alba had given birth to her own son, Thor, she had kept her role as second mother to Jonas.

A car horn sounded outside. They both frowned. Who could have come so early?

Katrin swept in, loud, red-cheeked, the many keys she always kept in her pockets jangling.

"My morning meeting was canceled, and the one after that, too, so I decided to come and see you both. I guess you know?"

"About Eyjafjöll?"

"It woke up after a hundred and eighty-seven years! How can anything wake up after sleeping for a hundred and eighty-seven years?"

"Or how can anything sleep for a hundred and eighty-seven years?" Jonas said.

The sisters looked at each other. Alba answered Katrin's question even before she had asked it. "I'll go tomorrow and see how things are, see if the cabin is in any danger."

"Thanks, Alba. If the cabin . . . "

Katrin fell silent, and Alba did not complete the sentence for her. They didn't dare admit to each other that if the house disappeared, it would be like a symbolic attack on their family.

Already there were only the two sisters left, each had only given birth to one child, and Jonas had little chance of . . .

"Will you come with me to my room? I'd like to show you the new underwear I bought in Paris."

Working for the International Committee of the Red Cross, Katrin traveled a lot, especially in Europe, from where she brought back gifts for her sister and her son.

"Oh, you two and your underwear!" Jonas grumbled. "That's really girls' stuff, that craze for lace . . . "

"Wait another two years, Jonas, and you'll see that girls' underwear is boys' stuff too."

They slipped upstairs to Katrin's room, opened the door, and sat down on the bed. Of course, Katrin had neither panties nor bra to unwrap. She had used their ritual code so that they could talk without being overheard.

"I'm very worried, Alba. Jonas had a whole bunch of tests at the hospital yesterday. This morning, I got an alarming report from Professor Gunnarsson: the cardiac malformation is getting worse. Jonas's heart could stop at any time."

"I realize that. At the age of fifteen, he isn't even capable of doing as much as an old man!"

"Gunnarsson says he needs a transplant as soon as possible. Otherwise . . . "

"Katrin, you've been going on and on about that for months! What can we do?"

"Jonas is on the waiting list but there are no donors. This is Iceland, a country with a population of three hundred thousand!"

"Yes, but the heart he gets doesn't necessarily have to be Icelandic. Remember what Professor Gunnarsson told us? That these days they can transport organs by plane . . . "

"That's the theory; in practice, it's different. I made inquiries: organs travel inside a country or from one country to a neighboring one. Never from one continent to another. Let alone from the continent to a remote island in the middle of nowhere . . . Jonas is going to die, Alba, if we don't do something now. I wonder . . . "

Alba realized that everything Katrin had been saying had been leading up to this. She knew her sister, knew how calculating she was. Good, kindhearted, well-intentioned, but calculating. Equipped with a strategist's brain, she conducted a private conversation as if it were a top-level professional meeting.

"Yes?" Alba insisted.

"We have to go to Europe. We have to take Jonas to Paris or Geneva. There are exponentially more chances of finding a compatible donor there."

At that moment, Alba grasped what her sister was telling her and had been hiding from her. "We? Let's be clear about this. Us means Jonas, you . . . and me?"

"Of course."

"You want me to come with you to Europe?"

"Yes, please. Just until Jonas gets his transplant. Because I'll still be traveling a lot."

Alba glared at her. "You're not the only person with work to do! I may not be an important international official, but I still have to earn my living."

"Alba, you're an artist, you're freer than I am. You can illustrate your children's books anywhere."

"That's true. But are you aware that I have a husband?"

Katrin bowed her head.

Alba insisted, "And that I also have a son, a teenager, who in his way causes me as many worries as Jonas?"

Katrin kept her head bowed, then murmured in a tearful voice, her true voice, her fragile voice, quite unlike her normal, authoritative political voice, "I'm not asking you this out of selfishness, Alba, or to prove to myself that I'm more important than you. I'm asking you because I won't be able to do it on my own. I'm asking you to make the operation possible. I'm asking you because you have the solution. For Jonas, Alba, only for him."

Alba thought of Jonas, and suddenly, the eternal conflict that opposed her to—and united her with—her beloved sister faded into the background. A sense of urgency made her throat tight. Jonas might die.

"I'll think about it." Alba kissed her sister on the forehead and stood up. "I promise I'll think about it. If anything happened to our Jonas, I . . . " Her voice trailed off, choked in her throat.

At that moment, Katrin knew that Alba had made up her mind.

*

"Have you noticed that I'm talking to you?"

Alba was standing in the doorway of the room, speaking to Thor, her fourteen-year-old son, who was staring at his computer without even glancing at his fingers as they moved rapidly, lightly, virtuosically, over the game console. Engaged in a virtual combat, he did not even seem to have noticed that his mother was there.

"What's your problem?" she went on in a more acrid tone. "Are you deaf? Are you stupid? Have you forgotten that you used to be able to speak Icelandic?"

Thor still did not react, eyes fixed on the screen, headphones on his ears. For months, Alba had only ever seen her son looking blue because, shut up all the time in this room, the only light he received was the turquoise light from his computer.

"Or have you left the human race? Have you mutated to join your digital world? Thor, I'm talking to you!"

This time, she had yelled.

He ignored her, still devoting all his energy to his game.

Reproaching herself for her reprimands, she resumed in a more even tone, although one still throbbing with irritation, "Thor, you've stopped being part of the family. I have the feeling I don't have a son anymore."

He threw himself back on his chair, yelling, "Shit!" Then, recovering, he leaned in toward the screen and started tapping more quickly on the keys, tense and irritable.

Alba's sharpness changed to irony. "Oh, my darling, what happened? Were you attacked by a green scaly monster? A medieval knight? A soldier from the planet Zarg?"

He pressed a button on his console and laughed with joy, triumphantly.

Alba pretended to applaud. "Congratulations, you've just won a little immunity, even though you're not quite immortal yet . . . Obviously, it's more useful to succeed in a world that doesn't exist than in this one, more important to zap fictitious enemies than to listen to your mother."

As he sang to himself, delighted with the nasty blow he had just inflicted on his opponents, she exploded, "I'm sorry we don't live in the United States, because there, I'd have the right to bear arms. Right now, I'd aim my gun at you, you'd be afraid that I'd shoot, you'd shit in your pants, and we'd finally be able to talk! Yes, Thor, with a gun pointed at your head, you'd be forced to look at your mother!"

A hand seized Alba by the waist, a mouth touched the back of her neck, and a pelvis was pressed against her buttocks.

"Alba, do you realize what you're saying?" Magnus whispered in her ear.

"Yes! Er . . . no."

How good he smelled . . . Knowing she was soon going to stop being angry, thanks to her husband's beneficial embrace, she spat out her last venom: "Anyway, even if I'm talking bullshit, I realize that better than he does."

They both gazed at the boy. Still plunged in a virtual universe, he was paying them no attention.

"We don't have a son, we have a fish in a tank. And I hate fish!"

"Alba, relax."

Under the pretext of calming her down, he starting stroking her breasts. His fingers were thick, but as they lingered over the most sensitive points, their touch was delicate.

How selfish he is! He doesn't want to calm me down, he just wants to fuck me. She was tempted to push him away when two things stopped her: the depressing sight of Thor frenetically pressing his thumbs on his console, and the smell of her man, an aroma of spicy ripe pear that, ever since the first day, had bound her to his powerful, muscular, sexually demanding body.

Like children hiding from their parents, they disappeared into their bedroom. In any case, even if the building was burning down, Thor would ignore her . . .

After their lovemaking and a quick shower, Alba had recovered the energy to confront daily life and announced cheerfully that she was going to make dinner.

*

When the smoked mutton with potatoes in white sauce was ready, she called Thor and Magnus.

Magnus came immediately, but Thor did not appear.

"Could you please check that your son isn't dead?"

Magnus dragged himself to the end of the corridor, ordered Thor to join them, came back, sat down at the table, and picked up his knife and fork. Confidently, Alba sat down opposite him and waited to serve.

"Did he hear you?"

"I think so."

"Did he understand?"

"I don't know."

"Doesn't it terrify you to have a zombie instead of a son?"

"It's the usual teenage rebelliousness. It'll sort itself out."

"Are you so sure? In our day, nobody had a computer."

"We had cigarettes, joints, alcohol . . . "

"Are you trying to say that our son is addicted to his computer?"

"In a way, yes."

"And aren't you going to do anything?"

He made an evasive grimace, groaned, then wearily grabbed the spoon and served himself.

"Aren't you going to wait for Thor?"

"I'm hungry."

"I thought we observed good manners in this household."

"Listen, Alba, Thor pisses me off, and frankly you're starting to piss me off too." With these resolute words, he lifted the meat to his mouth.

Taken aback by such vulgarity, Alba found a thousand thoughts jostling in her head: *When he wants to sleep with me, he's much more polite . . . He doesn't give a damn about our son's upbringing . . . The big ape thinks only of his stomach and his dick . . . There are times when I hate him . . . If I go to Thor's room, I'll hit that boy . . .*

She leaped up from her chair, went straight to the entrance of the apartment, opened the closet containing the electricity meter, and abruptly switched off the supply.

The apartment was plunged into darkness. There was a wonderful moment, a moment of great pleasure for Alba, when the place belonged to her again.

Then she heard Thor's whining moan: "Shit! What's going on?"

What a horrible voice! So nasal! He can't control it, it goes all shrill . . . That's not my son's voice.

"The power's gone off!"

And he's too lazy to get up off his chair, he just yells from his room!

"Hello! The power's gone off! Hello? Is there anyone there?"

Any normal child would call his mother and father. He just asks if anyone's there, as he was living with strangers.

"Hello? Isn't anyone going to fix it?"

Oh, fuck off, kid.

Thor emerged from his room and came down the dark corridor. When he saw his mother, he sighed, "About time."

"About time for what?"

"About time you fixed it."

"What do you think I'm here for?"

Thor's mouth opened. *He really is completely dumb.*

"Yes, Thor, you heard me," she raged. "Who exactly do you think I am? Your mother, or just the person who provides the electricity, pays the bill, and goes to press the button so you can escape into your game?"

He stood there dumbfounded. She decided to take advantage of the moment. "Come to the table. I have something to ask you and your father."

He made an obscene noise, then stubbornly approached the meter and made to press the green button. She grabbed his arm to stop him.

"Don't touch, it's mine!"

"Are you crazy?"

"How would you know? I might have gone crazy ages ago. You haven't looked at me or talked to me in months."

He tried to reach the meter again. This time, she slapped his hand. He jumped back.

"You . . . you hit me!" he said, rubbing his wrist.

"Oh, I'm glad you noticed."

"But you've never hit me before!"

"And maybe I was wrong all these years. Shall we do it again?"

He moved his other hand around in a circle close to his forehead, as if to say that she was losing her mind, and walked back down the corridor.

"Thor, where are you going?"

"To get my things from my room."

"Thor, I have something to discuss with you and your father."

"I'm not staying in a house where I'm going to be hit."

Alba ran to the dining room. "Do something!" she yelled at Magnus.

Glumly, Magnus cried out in a lazy, insufficiently firm voice, "Where are you going, Thor?"

"To Grandpa's."

Alba grabbed her husband by the shoulder. "Stop him! Tell him not to do it."

Magnus sighed. "Your mother and I don't really agree . . . "

Thor walked the length of the corridor and hissed at them, "Too bad. Bye!"

The door slammed.

Alba and Magnus were still in darkness.

She turned her rage on him. "Congratulations! What a father! Such authority!"

"Leave me alone, Alba. If you think you're any better—a hysterical woman who threatens to buy a gun and shoot her son, and then goes and cuts off the electricity! I've never seen such pathetic behavior!"

He stood up, knocking his chair over as he did so.

"Where are you going? Magnus, I forbid you to leave! Where are you going?"

He put on his down jacket, then turned back to her. "To the sports club. I'll grab a sandwich over there. Then I'll bust a gut on the mat, just to forget this hellhole we're living in."

The door slammed again.

Alba collapsed onto her chair, her head in her hands. "Oh, Jonas, how happy the two of us are going to be in Europe . . . "

*

The next day, driving along the coast road was enough to cheer her up. As her car reached the hills, Alba had the feeling she was hugging the light, merging with nature.

Around her was a symphony of blues: the ultramarine of the ocean, the periwinkle of the sky, the opal of the ice, the cobalt of the streams, the slate of the rocks, the turquoise of the tar and, finally, dominant although subtle, the almost almond shade of the snow.

The radio was broadcasting news of the eruption: it was still going on, there were more and more shafts of lava, but, for the moment, it didn't seem that the danger was getting any worse. When she left Route 1, which encircled the whole of Iceland, she moved onto roads where the snow had not been completely cleared, and several times her wheels almost got bogged down. She went as high as she possibly could, then, when she realized she was going to be stuck, switched off the engine and resolved to continue on foot.

After some twenty paces, she noticed her cell phone wasn't in her pocket. Retracing her steps, she looked inside the car, and searched between the seats: nothing.

She let out a laugh. What a godsend! Nobody would be able to contact her today. She was free and clear! Thanks to her forgetfulness, she was going to be really alone. For now, she belonged to no one but herself.

Lightheartedly, she resumed her ascent, rediscovering the elation of childhood, the feeling of being a tiny speck in the vastness of nature, unattached, impossible to contact, in danger . . . It was delightful.

Her heart beat faster with the joy of it.

Snow, stone, moss, mud, crushed lava: the ground echoed with many different familiar noises beneath her walking shoes.

An hour later, she came within sight of the cabin, huddled like a nest in the rocky landscape. There it stood, untouched.

At that moment, Alba told herself that she had deliberately exaggerated the danger from the eruption, which was actually quite some distance from here. She had probably just wanted an excuse to get away as soon as possible . . .

A breeze caressed her face, more a breath of air than a gust of wind. She stopped to contemplate the landscape around her. Filling her lungs deeply, she had the conviction that she was in her place. Iceland wasn't the end of the world, as Americans and Europeans thought, but the point where the world culminated, a land fed by the winds from the North Pole, Africa, Alaska, and Russia, a land desired by migrating birds, terns, ducks, and wild geese, a land where floating logs drifting from Norway landed after a long journey.

The house was waiting for her, its blood-red façade contrasting with the grim hills.

As she slid the heavy old key into the lock, Alba noticed that the paint was flaking and peeling. That would be a great way to spend the summer . . . She'd ask Jonas to come with her, and they'd have a lot of fun refurbishing this antique—if Jonas got his transplant, that is.

The cold had shrunk the wood, and it took time for the door to yield. At last, Alba went inside, and rediscovered the smell of the oil used for the lamps, the hams hanging from hooks above the sink, the hay in the mattresses that were taken out in the summer and on which they lay for hours enjoying the polar day.

For fear that she would die of cold, she lit a large fire then set about doing a little tidying. Without even realizing it, she devoted the rest of the day to this.

If she hadn't felt the need to clean the hanging lamp, she

wouldn't have become aware that the sky had been getting darker for hours. As usual when she was here, she hadn't seen the afternoon pass! Was it because she was back in her childhood days, that time that seems to last forever, like a reflection of eternity?

Still she didn't move, taking as much advantage as she could of this respite, isolated by the weak, reddish glow of the flame within the shadowy vastness.

At eight in the evening, she turned everything off, checked several times that the fire had gone out completely, then reluctantly closed the door and walked back to her car. The path was less passable than when she had come, because, in this inky darkness, she couldn't see where she was putting her feet.

Once in the car, as soon as she had warmed herself, she switched on the radio and set off.

There was more news of the eruption. The authorities had announced that they were lifting the ban on access to the volcano, a sign that the situation was improving.

Alba drove idly, more concerned with daydreaming than with speed. Since the landscape was hidden in the darkness, she let her thoughts parade in front of her. She imagined herself in Geneva—Katrin had many contacts at Red Cross headquarters—in an apartment overlooking the lake, pampering Jonas after his operation. When you came down to it, her sister was right: it wouldn't be any problem professionally, she could draw just as well in Switzerland as in Reykjavík. As for her husband and her son . . . why should she give up on traveling because of them? They didn't deserve it. She laughed as she thought of new names for them: Thor the Lazy and Magnus the Cowardly.

Back in the city, just to assert her independence, she lingered over a creamy coffee in a bar that was open late, then at last made up her mind to go home. Had Thor and Magnus even noticed she was gone? Magnus probably, because he had had to make dinner, but Thor?

She was pulling open the heavy glass door leading into the lobby of her building when she heard a car door slam, followed by hurried foosteps and her name being called.

"Alba!"

Turning, she saw Katrin, her face streaked with tears, coming straight toward her, tottering slightly.

"Alba . . . Alba . . . "

Katrin collapsed in her arms, unable to get the slightest word out.

Alba realized that something had happened to Jonas. Was he sick? Was he . . . dead? My God, as long as his heart hadn't given out!

She hugged her sister, already consoling her, and stammered, "Tell me . . . tell me . . . please . . . tell me . . . Katrin, my dear, I beg you . . . tell me."

Katrin, who was usually so self-possessed, tried several times, but couldn't.

Preparing herself for the worst, Alba started to weep silently . . . Poor Jonas . . . He would never become an adult . . . Had he suffered? Had he been conscious? Oh, Jonas and his beautiful lips . . . Jonas and his loving attention to her . . . It was horrible.

Katrin broke free, caught her breath, looked hard at her younger sister, and, with a superhuman effort of will, murmured, "Thor's dead."

Alba froze. "I beg your pardon?"

"Your son had an accident this morning," Katrin went on. "As he was leaving your father-in-law's house, the wheel of his moped skidded on a patch of ice. He was thrown off and hit his head on a post. He wasn't wearing his helmet . . . He . . . he died instantly."

Alba glared at her sister. Her eyes were saying, *You're wrong. If anyone was supposed to die, it was Jonas, not Thor.*

Then she opened the door, walked unsteadily across the

lobby and, before she had even set foot on the bottom step of the staircase, fainted.

*

For three days, Alba wouldn't talk to anyone. She stayed in her room, sitting on the quilt of her bed, curtains drawn, asking Magnus to keep the door closed and not let any visitors in or put through any phone calls to her.

When, on several occasions, Magnus came in and tried to talk to her, she turned her head away.

The fifth time this happened, he protested, "Look, Alba, I've also just lost my son. Our son. I need to share my grief with you."

At the word "grief," Alba emerged from her torpor and stared hard at Magnus, his square shoulders, his vigorous torso, his heavily-veined, bull-like neck; instinctively, she pushed away the hands stroking her thighs, disapproved of her husband's red eyes—aesthetically speaking, tears didn't suit a red-blooded man with brown hair—then sighed desolately, "I don't have anything to share, Magnus."

"You hate me."

"For what?"

"I have no idea."

"I don't hate you, Magnus. Just go."

These four sentences having exhausted her, she closed her eyes.

No, she wouldn't share Magnus's grief because she didn't feel any grief. She was still in a state of shock. Surprise was still distilling its poison, paralyzing both her emotions and her thoughts.

All she could do was wait for Thor's funeral.

And so she waited.

To be present, to escort Thor to his final resting place: that was her one aim.

Apart from that task . . .

Several times during those three days, Katrin knocked timidly at the door of her sister's room and implored her to let her in.

Each time, Alba, with a sudden spurt of energy, leaped out of bed and turned the key. Especially not Katrin! Alba didn't know why, but not Katrin! What made it worse was that Katrin tried to argue with her through the door . . . Anyway, with those foam rubber plugs stuck in her ears, Alba couldn't even hear her . . .

Often, when she woke after having dozed off, the image of Jonas would come into her mind. She immediately dismissed it. No, she shouldn't be thinking about Jonas but about Thor.

It didn't work, though . . . It was as if her memories had been torn from her, as if she had never had a son. Strange, wasn't it?

In three days, nothing improved: she still couldn't think about Thor, but an unpleasant feeling swept through her every time her mind turned to Jonas.

What shocked her was that the only thing she felt was annoyance. Her grief was behind a transparent wall, a thick pane of glass along which she walked; there were times when she wanted to break the glass so that she could really suffer; at other times, she simply gazed placidly at the grief she couldn't feel.

*

At the funeral, wrapped in a scarf and hidden behind huge dark glasses, she clung to Magnus's hand and mutely played her role. For just one moment, when the undertaker's men moved the coffin closer to the grave, that hole of black earth with its snow-lined edges struck her as obscene and she was afraid that Thor would be cold in there. Then she looked up and saw a gull flying across the sky, and her mind went blank again.

As she got back to her car, she stopped, suddenly distracted by an absence: Jonas hadn't attended the ceremony. How was it possible that he hadn't come to the funeral of Thor, the cousin he worshiped?

She went up to Katrin, who was standing by her car, her back erect.

"Where's Jonas?"

"My dear, there are so many things I have to tell you . . . "

"Yes, yes. Where's Jonas?"

Katrin grabbed her sister by the shoulders, overjoyed at renewing contact with her. "You're speaking to me at last!"

"Where's Jonas?"

"Do you really want me to tell you?"

"Well?"

"He's in the hospital. They operated on him. The transplant seems to be taking."

Alba felt a warm sensation suffuse her: the delight she would have known if she had heard this weeks earlier. "I'm very glad, Katrin. Yes, I'm really glad he's saved."

The word "saved" triggered something. All the feelings she had been suppressing re-emerged thanks to that single syllable.

"Saved" told her that Jonas was going to live . . .

"Saved" told her that Thor was dead.

Like an eruption of lava, joy and sadness rose inside her and joined, exploding violently into sobs. Alba was shaken with both happiness and sorrow.

Katrin hugged her, as did Magnus. They were both relieved to see that she was back in the land of the living.

*

That evening, Alba asked Katrin if she could see her nephew.

As they were approaching intensive care, a huge nurse with

a mustache on her upper lip and teeth as small as whalebones blocked the entrance and asked them to wait for twenty minutes until the medical team had finished.

They went to the cafeteria on that floor, a room with orange walls that wouldn't have looked out of place in a kindergarten. Katrin told her sister the circumstances of the operation:

"They called us at five o'clock in the afternoon and told us to come straight to the hospital. Jonas and I only had the time it took us to get there to think about what was going to happen. What's there to think about anyway? They tell you you're getting a new organ, that they're going to open your chest, saw into your bones, take your heart out, sew in somebody else's— in other words, a risky procedure. They tell you that even if the operation goes well, there can be complications in the weeks that follow, when they determine if your body has accepted the new heart or not. Still, when you think about it, that hurry isn't so bad . . . It saves you hours of worrying."

"How did Jonas behave?"

"He was terrified, but he hid it well. He tried to give me the impression he was going for a routine test. I respected his courage and I behaved the way he did. We laughed and joked up until the last moment."

"Up until the last moment?"

"When they administered the anesthetic."

Katrin clenched her jaws, preferring not to continue— while the surgeons were operating, she had found it so hard to overcome her anxiety that she had thrown up several times in the corridor and had had to be sedated.

"How is he?"

"Fine, apparently. For the moment, he's still intubated, and hooked up to all kinds of machines, but there's a gleam in his eyes and he's said a few words."

"What did he say?"

"He asked me when you were coming."

Alba wiped her eyes. Jonas's pure affection moved her all the more now that he was all she had left.

Katrin understood that and squeezed her hand. "Drink your coffee, darling. I'll go see what they're up to and come back for you."

Alba nodded then said slowly, "Don't worry, I'll be okay, I won't burst into tears."

"Thanks, Alba."

Katrin walked away. As she was about to leave the room, she turned and said, "Especially as Jonas doesn't know . . . "

"Doesn't know what?"

"About Thor."

Alba gave a start.

Seeing her reaction, Katrin was forced to explain. "I . . . I didn't have the courage to inflict that on him when he woke up . . . I wanted to protect him . . . You know how sensitive he is—how would he have reacted? We'll tell him later, when we're certain he's recovered." She hesitated, unsure of her sister's approval. "Don't you think?"

"Yes," Alba replied in a neutral voice. "Of course."

Katrin disappeared into the bowels of the intensive care unit with its green fluorescent lighting.

Once alone, Alba raised an eyebrow. *They think I'm going to say hello to my nephew and hide from him the fact that I'm in mourning for my son? I have to tell him straight away. Otherwise, it won't be me who's seeing Jonas, it'll be someone else. I won't lend myself to that farce.*

In three minutes, she put her thoughts in order, so that she could be ready for when Katrin returned.

There was a sudden flurry of movement in the corridor. Four male nurses and an intern came racing along. Like a motorcycle escort, the first two nurses were clearing the way, the third held a steel box at the end of his arm, the last brought up the rear. At their side, the intern was running, eyes fixed on the box as if it was a priceless treasure.

They turned at the corner, beneath a sign reading *Operating Room.*

The scene had unfolded as if in secret, but it intrigued Alba. She turned to a nurse's aide who was drinking a carrot juice in the cafeteria. "What was that?" she asked.

"They were bringing in an organ for transplant."

"Where did it come from?"

"That's confidential, madam. The system is regulated like an Olympic race. The organ can be kept for a few hours in liquid nitrogen, but they still hurry, because every minute counts."

Alba thanked her and let her thoughts wander. So a human being had to die for another to live! One tragedy, one comedy. Like the events she was living through, Thor dying, Jonas getting a transplant . . .

She sat up, her temples damp, shivers down her spine.

"Thor! Jonas!"

It was like a thunderbolt: they had given Jonas Thor's heart. Disconcerted, she turned that thought over and over, then made an effort to dismiss it. "No, that's rubbish!"

Katrin came back into the room. "They'll be finished in five minutes. I'll just have a word with the surgeon and I'll be back to fetch you."

"Wait a minute! You never told me when they did the transplant."

Upset by the question, Katrin stammered, "The transplant? Er . . . four days ago."

"Wednesday?"

"Er . . . yes . . . Wednesday . . . "

"The day . . . "

"Yes?"

"The day Thor died?"

Katrin blinked, said, "Yes," and walked out.

The cafeteria had lost its color and texture: the walls seemed vague, spattered with the red of blood. Alba grabbed her cell phone.

"Magnus, I—"

"Are you at the hospital? How's Jonas?"

"I haven't seen him yet. Magnus, I'm not calling you about that. Did . . ."

She couldn't utter the words.

"Yes, Alba?"

If she came out with it, she foresaw that she would be plunged into a world where nothing would be as it had been before.

"Alba, I'm listening . . ."

She had to say it. She had to be brave.

"Magnus, did they remove an organ from Thor?"

The image of a man opening her son's chest and rooting about inside hit her hard.

Silence fell, a silence that lasted. Then Magnus's cavernous voice resumed with forced gusto, "It's possible. You know, Thor had a donor's card after one of his teachers had talked to the class about these things. When I was asked, I told them they should do what he would have wanted."

"Why didn't you consult me?"

"I tried to reach you all day, Alba, from morning to night! Don't forget you left your cell phone behind in the apartment."

"All the same . . . a decision of that importance . . ."

"I called you dozens of times, Alba!"

"Yes, but . . ."

"What difference would it have made? You would have respected Thor's decision. You would have said the same, Alba, maybe even before I did. I know you, I know your beliefs."

"So what happened?"

"What do you mean?"

"Did they remove an organ from Thor?"

Magnus paused for a few seconds, then replied, "If you think about it, there's a good chance they did. Thor was brain dead because of the trauma to his skull. There were no lesions on the rest of his body."

"So they used him . . . What did they take?"

"I don't know."

"Yes, you do!"

"No, and we'll never know."

"I don't believe you."

"It's the law, Alba. They asked me a standard question and I gave them a standard answer. What happened next is no concern of ours."

"Oh, really? You mean I don't have a right to know if they cut my son up and what they did with him? This is a nightmare!"

Magnus hesitated, grunted, then resumed in a calm voice, "Where are you now, darling? I'll come and get you."

*

Apart from Magnus and Katrin, nobody understood why Alba refused for several weeks to visit her nephew in the hospital. They were all surprised that a godmother who, until then, had never spent two days without seeing her godson could have broken off such an exceptional relationship. Some thought it was a kind of jealousy—one child dies, another recovers—but as soon as they put forward this hypothesis, her nearest and dearest defended her, saying that such pettiness wasn't in her character.

Alba had resumed her work. "I have a children's book to finish," she would mutter to anyone who tried to engage her in conversation. Although it was true that she had to finish the illustrations for a story by Andersen, she was glad that painting served as a barrier against intruders and isolated her in her thoughts.

Over her pots and brushes, she brooded on her anger. Without respite, from morning to evening, she came back again and again to the thing that wounded her: her son's heart had been put in her nephew's body without her being asked. Her sister suspected it, but Magnus didn't give a damn. "A matter of principle," he kept saying! They're such cowards, these men, when they forget their scruples and cling to their principles!

At night, she would search endlessly on the internet, reading the views and explanations of politicians, ethical committees, psychiatrists, and patients' associations. Was there a way of finding out what happened to the organs? In spite of the legal ban, had there ever been a court case that had allowed a parent to break that intolerable silence?

Magnus viewed all this agitation with a skeptical eye. "Why do you want to know what they did with our son's body?"

"First of all, my son's body is still my son. Secondly, when they removed his organs, he was alive."

"You're confusing brain death and the heart stopping."

"I'm not confusing anything. His heart was beating. They tore it out of him."

At last, she reached the ultimate conclusion to all this hairsplitting: they had killed Thor so that Jonas could survive.

Losing his temper, Magnus brought her down to earth. "His skull had been smashed in, his other organs were surviving mechanically, they would have stopped soon."

"Are you a doctor?"

"More than you are. You don't understand a thing."

"I don't give a damn about understanding, I want to know!"

"All you'll do is poison your life."

"It's already poisoned."

To put an end to these scenes that could easily have continued until dawn, Magnus would slam the door and go to his
sports club.

Their marriage was deteriorating under the pressure. Aware
that she was responsible, she took pride in the fact. "At least I
don't compromise, I search for the truth."

Some evenings, though, she managed to assuage her grief,
or rather Magnus's expert hands managed to do so, the intoxicating smell of his skin, his brown hair, his animal tenderness.
Alas, as soon as they had climaxed and their bodies moved
apart, she would think of Thor and feel guilty.

Guilty of what?

Of living for a few minutes as if her son wasn't dead.

In any case, that was what she thought she was guilty of . . .

*

Jonas had been moved from intensive care to the ward for
convalescent cardiac patients. Ever since he had heard about
his cousin's death, he had been writing daily e-mails to his aunt
in which he related in a humorous manner his stay in the hospital, trying to amuse her with portraits of those around him—
patients and medical staff—then venturing, in discreet words,
to understand and share her grief. Touched by the first two
messages, Alba now deleted them without even opening them.
From those first e-mails, she had kept only one sentence:
"Another heart is beating in my chest, but I'm still the same."
Those words haunted her. It seemed to her they were killing
Thor for the second time, because they denied that the presence of his heart had made any substantial difference to Jonas.
The little bastard! How could he be so selfish?

After all these weeks shut away, she delivered her illustrations for the Andersen story and saw, from the dismayed expressions of the publisher and her assistants, that the results didn't greatly appeal to them.

"Don't you like them?"

"A bit dark, aren't they? Not like your usual style."

"That's how I see things. Before, I was only a silly woman who believed in happiness."

"We . . . we loved the silly woman's drawings."

"And I loved being silly. But that's over now."

Having fulfilled her commission, Alba was able to devote her days to her investigation. Was Thor's heart in Jonas's chest? By collecting and collating all the information she could find, she didn't unearth the truth but did see two ways to get at it: a legal way, and an illegal way. The legal way meant making an appointment at the transplant center, the illegal meant joining a group of activists, Liberaria, who were planning to break the rules.

Her obsession hadn't completely obliterated her judgment, so she first went to the transplant center, where one of the administrators, Mr. Sturluson, greeted her from behind his chrome desk. Around him were a dozen posters boasting of health recovered, each bearing a photograph of a transplant patient in overly bright colors, the kind you see in travel agency posters.

As she sat down opposite Mr. Sturluson, his three-day growth of dark beard reminded her of Magnus—another Basque probably, all the dark-haired men in Iceland were descended from Basque sailors!—a thinner, less handsome version of Magnus, which set alarm bells ringing inside her: *Don't lose your temper, don't be as hysterical as Magnus says you are.*

So she calmly explained her situation: as the mother of a child who had agreed—as had she and her husband, she made clear—to be an organ donor, she wanted to know what had happened.

"You made the right choice, madam, and I congratulate you. Society needs people like you."

"What happened after that?"

"We made a wise use of your permission. I have no doubt a life was saved thanks to your generosity."

"'No doubt' . . . But why can't I be sure?"

"We aren't authorized to go into details, madam."

"But you have the details in your possession?"

Mr. Sturluson indicated his computer. "We have that information, of course. For medical reasons, we have to be able to know where the organs went."

"Then tell me."

"I'm not authorized."

"Please."

He shook his head, the result of which was to project dandruff onto his charcoal gray jacket.

Her hand brushed the computer. "Look, it's here, in this box. Just press the right key and you'll set my mind at rest."

"Why are you so determined to know, madam?"

She was taken aback. Why? It was necessary to her. Essential. At that moment, her whole being boiled down to that one thing.

"Do I ask you why you're alive, sir?"

"I beg your pardon?"

"What I mean is that people usually fail to answer the important questions. And yet you can answer this question for me. I'm listening."

"I took an oath, madam."

She sat back on her chair, brows knitted, nostrils quivering. "Do you think it's normal that a bureaucrat whose only concern is his monthly salary can hold on to vital information about my son, while his mother, who gave birth to him, raised him, loved him, and is now mourning him, can't access it?"

"Normal or not, madam, it's the law."

She felt she was going to kill him.

He sensed it too.

For a brief lapse of time, Alba's eyes shone with a murderous flame. Everything seemed simple to her: she would strangle him, then open his computer. Not complicated, was it?

Sweat broke out on Sturluson's forehead.

A homicidal joy was boiling up in Alba. Ten more seconds and she would put her hand around this awful man's throat.

A security guard entered without warning.

"Did you call me? Is there a problem?"

He was more than six feet tall and his forearms were thicker than Alba's thighs. She realized that Sturluson had pressed an alarm button.

"No, Ghemar, it's all right," Sturluson sighed. "Please see the lady out. She's upset because she's just suffered a terrible bereavement. Thank you for coming to see me, madam, and, once again, I congratulate you."

She felt a strong desire to spit in his face as she left the room, but then she realized that she would only be lowering herself if she paid any more attention to a mere cog in the bureaucratic machine.

"You could at least shave," she said as she went out. "Given how ugly you already are . . . "

*

She'd had enough of playing with the pawns. It was the whole chessboard she had to attack now.

That afternoon, she contacted the people on the Liberaria website. This revolutionary association had the same aims as she did: to denounce the state, to fight excessive rules, to allow individuals to take possession of their own lives, to combat all forms of secrecy.

After several phone conversations with the leader of the

group, known as Erik the Red, who, like her, wished to subvert the principles of the world, she was invited to an informal meeting at the Mermaid Café one Monday evening. According to Erik the Red, there would be some twenty people at the meeting.

When she opened the grimy door of the café, she saw only four people: an unusually short man, a pretty redhead who was biting her nails, a fair-haired man thinner than a matchstick, and a punk girl with green hair. She was just checking her watch to make sure she hadn't gotten the wrong time when the short man stood up, dry as a smoked herring, and signaled to her with his childlike hand.

"Erda?" he asked.

"Yes," Alba said—that was the name she had adopted for her research on the internet.

"I'm Erik the Red," he said, motioning for her to sit down.

She slipped onto the bench and they started talking over a beer. Cautiously, they exchanged a few general remarks on the dictatorship of the state, just to make sure they were on the same wavelength, then the debate warmed up. As he spoke—passionately, lyrically—Erik the Red lived up to his pseudonym; if, on entering, Alba hadn't seen any resemblance between this puny fellow and the tenth-century Viking hero, banished from Norway then from Iceland, who had discovered the virgin coasts of Greenland, she could now glimpse the shade of that ambitious soul in him.

The members' individual experiences explained their commitment: Erik the Red had seen his father blow his brains out after a drastic tax adjustment, the punk girl had wandered from orphanage to reform school, the thin, fair-haired man had been arrested several times for stealing documents while investigating corruption among members of parliament. But it was Vilma, the redhead with the creamy complexion, who moved Alba the most, since both shared an identical history—the fragile Vilma had lost her daughter not long before and couldn't find out what had become of her organs.

This unexpected similarity moved Alba deeply. At any other time, she wouldn't have paid any attention to this young woman. She would have been repelled by trifling things—her chewed nails, her yellow teeth—but now she rose above this aesthetic approach to the world and concentrated on Vilma's personality. It was obvious the woman was suffering as much as she was. Whenever Vilma mentioned her daughter, her fruity voice shook, threatening to break, and brought her audience to the verge of tears. Alba sobbed shamelessly . . . It was as if Vilma were speaking for her.

Urged to tell her story, Alba told them about her encounter with Sturluson. They sympathized, they took offense, and all regretted that she hadn't had time to kill the man. Vilma was staring at her. This response gratified Alba—she hadn't dared tell Magnus what had happened at the transplant center.

"I'll help you," the fair-haired man, who was known as Whistle, suggested. "I'll try to hack into the website."

"Can you do that?"

Vilma and Alba were taken aback. Flattered, Whistle nodded.

Alba went home galvanized: she had finally found support, she had finally met people shocked by injustice. Especially Vilma . . .

Before going to bed, she sent her a text. *Pleased to have met you. Shall we stay friends?* A few seconds later, she had a reply: *I can't do without your friendship. See you tomorrow. Love.*

*

Alba began a life in parallel to her official life. Without saying anything to Magnus or Katrin, she saw Vilma every day.

The two women understood each other, listened to each other, supported each other, wept together.

At the hospital, Jonas was making good progress: his body was tolerating the transplanted organ. Puzzled not to see his godmother, he sent ever more urgent e-mails, then sent Katrin and Magnus as ambassadors.

"What has he done to you?" her sister and husband asked her.

Alba found it harder and harder to justify her refusal, especially as she couldn't tell them openly that her nephew's fate depended on her investigation: either he had stolen Thor's heart and she would hate him until the day she died, or he was alive thanks to a stranger's heart and she would once again be able to embrace him.

Pursued by the whole family, she resolved to write a letter that belied her real emotions. Pretending to still feel what she felt before, to still be the affectionate godmother she had once been, she wrote a wonderful text, vibrant with love and overflowing with compassion, which moved Jonas, Katrin, and Magnus deeply—she sent them all copies—and moved her too.

Having obtained this reprieve, she went to see Vilma, her new sister, who allowed her to express what she actually felt.

One afternoon, because there were too many people in the café and Vilma really wanted to see her drawings, she took her home with her.

Open-mouthed and wide-eyed, Vilma examined every object, asking their provenance or their price, unable to conduct a normal conversation. Flattered, Alba let her rhapsodize.

Outside Thor's room, Alba came to a halt. "I haven't set foot in here since he went."

Knowing that Magnus had tidied the room, she dreaded seeing the result. Whatever he had done, it would hurt her: either he had kept it in its original state and she would enter a grim mausoleum, or he had wiped out all traces of Thor and the boy would be snatched from her a second time.

"Curious," Vilma said. "I always have my daughter's things with me. Here, look, I have her notebook in my bag. How can you live next to a room that's all boarded up?"

Alba thought about "Bluebeard," the Perrault story she had once illustrated, in which a young bride cannot bear her husband hiding a room from her and, in trying to find out the truth, narrowly escapes death.

"For now, yes."

Sensing that she shouldn't insist, Vilma turned her attention to an old key hanging from a hook on the wall in the corridor. "What's this?"

They went back to the living room, and Alba happily told her about the cabin, her childhood house in the south, not far from Eyjafjöll.

They were startled by a noise. Magnus had come home earlier than expected. They stood up, blushing, as if caught in the act.

"Hello, darling." As Alba was still frozen, he insisted, "Aren't you going to introduce me?"

Alba shook off her lethargy. "Magnus, this is my new friend Vilma."

Magnus threw an intrigued look at the slightly built Vilma, a look in which there was a touch of anxiety: it wasn't common for Alba, who wasn't very sociable, and was so attached to her sister and her godson, to bring "new friends" home.

Vilma, for her part, gave a broad smile, touched her hair coquettishly, and even wiggled her hips slightly. This gesture surprised Alba so much, she thought she must have been mistaken.

"I'll see you out, Vilma."

"Nice to have met you," Magnus muttered, heading for the bathroom.

By the time they had gone back down the three flights of stairs, Vilma was once again the suffering, tearful, inconsolable mother Alba had been seeing since that first visit to the Mermaid Café. She was reassured: after all, Vilma and she had so many things in common, it was only natural they would like the same type of men.

Watching her walk away along the sidewalks heavy with gray snow, Alba realized that, even though she told Vilma her most private sorrows, she had never told her about Jonas or revealed that she suspected her godson of having stolen her son's heart.

Once back upstairs, she implored Magnus, "Please don't ask me for any explanations."

"That's a pity," he sighed. "I'd have liked to know how you came to meet a redheaded mouse."

A day or two earlier, she would have picked a quarrel with him—they weren't supposed to laugh since Thor had died. That evening, though, Magnus's irony suited her too much for her to criticize him.

*

In the morning, Katrin burst in on them. She put some cookies on the table to justify her intrusion, said she would make breakfast, threw an embarrassed glance at Magnus—whose privates, though at rest, swelled his underpants flatteringly—then said to Alba, "My sister, I have a favor to ask you."

Katrin had uttered these words as she might have said, "My sister, I have an order to give you."

"Jonas is leaving hospital tomorrow, and I have to go to Geneva for a crucial meeting. Matters of world strategy, cooperation of the Red Cross with the Red Crescent, etc. I'm chairing it, so I absolutely have to attend. You'll have to get Jonas settled in at home and take care of him. Don't worry, Liv will make the meals and do the shopping. With both Liv and you there, we'll be able to keep an eye on him. Liv agrees. What do you think?"

As usual when faced with one of her elder sister's demands, Alba was struck dumb. Katrin was so domineering, she always presented her with a *fait accompli*. It was as if she were the only person in the world who couldn't take care of her family because of pressing engagements, and she seemed to find it natural that her sister should make herself as freely available as Liv, a housekeeper whom she actually paid.

"Do I have any choice?" Alba said, stirring her tea.

For forty years, that had been her way of saying yes to her elder sister.

*

She walked to the cardiology department, dreading her reunion with Jonas. Would he ask her to explain why she had stayed away? What would she reply? Would they still understand each other? Would she be able to conceal her grief, her anger, her frustration? She had changed so much since Thor's death! And Jonas had matured since his operation . . . Two strangers were about to meet, doomed to play at a familiarity that no longer existed.

As soon as she crossed the threshold, a kind of miracle took place: the luminous grace with which they had always been surrounded now flooded over them. They kissed, joked, laughed, and chatted, drunk with happiness.

Because Jonas made no reference to the past few weeks, it was a simple, warm, immensely sweet occasion. Overjoyed to see his aunt again, Jonas couldn't stop talking. He was radiant. As for Alba, she had the feeling she was going back to the old days, the days when everything had been wonderful. There was even a fleeting moment of amnesia when, amused by her godson's clever reflections, she thought that when she got home she would find Thor stubbornly glued to his screen.

Doctors and nurses came in to arrange Jonas's departure. As usual, he had charmed everyone. "Come back to see us, even if you aren't sick," they all said. It made Alba feel proud—proud to be the godmother of such a charismatic young man.

She drove him carefully to his mother's house, which was half an hour from Reykjavík. Jonas was like a convict just released from prison, marveling at the light, the colors, the tiny changes in the climate since he had been admitted to the hospital. Winter was losing its grip but spring had not yet established itself. From time to time, the wind rushed into the empty spaces, bringing flurries of snow with it.

They arrived to a lunch of dried fish and rye cakes prepared by Liv. Exhausted and overexcited, Jonas collapsed on the couch with a plate in his hand and switched on the television.

The screen showed a series of explosions above a glacier, then a colossal column of smoke reaching up into the sky. After a lull, the volcano Eyjafjöll had become active again, in fact, more active than ever. Although the first eruption hadn't caused any major damage or claimed any victims, the second was destroying roads, farms, and power lines.

Their first impulse was to worry about the cabin, then the flood of images carried them away and they stared at the TV screen, hypnotized by the godlike action of the earth.

Since the previous day, nature had been producing a spectacle far more fearsome, more terrifying, and more masterly than the best Hollywood special effects.

Everything had begun with an ice break. When the volcano started erupting, the heat of the magma had melted the lower layers of the glacier. The water had accumulated, held in by the rocks and kept down by the frozen icecap. When the pressure had become too great, this natural lid had burst open, releasing enormous quantities of liquid. By now, the jets were rising into the sky, laden with rocks, particles, and gas. While the heaviest elements fell back down immediately, bombarding the area round the volcano with stones, the lightest formed a plume of dust a few miles high. Lightning flashed from it, capricious and wild, liberating the electricity caused by the clash of molecules.

"Do you realize, Alba, that whenever something memorable happens to us, Eyjafjöll does something? It spits when we leave each other, it explodes when we meet again. What we have between us is cosmic."

Alba smiled in agreement.

The day continued. To avoid the transplanted heart being rejected, the medical team had lowered Jonas's immune reactions, which meant that he had to be protected against germs, viruses and bacteria.

Alba and Jonas resumed their traditions: card games, playing piano duets, reading side by side, and watching films.

"Aren't you drawing anything right now, Auntie?"

Alba shook her head. Drawing meant opening the door to her soul, which was so murky she was determined to keep it secret. A curious phenomenon had taken place inside her: she had divided herself. A surface Alba coexisted with another, buried Alba. On the outside, she was living happily with her nephew, affable, dynamic, even-tempered; inside, an angry woman looked at the boy with suspicion, condemning everything he said, seeing some act of treachery beneath the most insignificant word, plotting her vengeance, waiting for the hour when he would be punished. As soon as she could be certain that he had stolen Thor's heart, that her son had been murdered for his sake, she would take her revenge.

That was what the demonic Alba was pondering while the angelic Alba joked with her nephew. Both lived together beneath the same exterior.

But for the moment, there was no way. Whistle said he had another mission to carry out first. The waiting was becoming intolerable . . .

*

One evening, when Jonas had fallen asleep watching a Frank Capra comedy, Alba bent over him. Was there a way to see if Thor's heart was beating inside Jonas? A mother should be able to spot that. No need to use her senses . . . her instinct would tell her. She just had to be beside his body and open her mind to her emotions.

She stared at the boy.

A feeling of intense familiarity overcame her. There in front of her was more than her nephew. There was something in Jonas that came from elsewhere, something that animated the curl of his lips, agitated his girlish eyelashes, ran through the delicate veins that crisscrossed his milk-white arms, made his narrow chest rise and fall. That something was her son. What was best in this patient named Jonas, what was healthy and essential, was Thor. Thor had been killed to prolong the existence of this useless invalid. There was no doubt about it.

Alba decided to have done with it once and for all! There was no way she could smile at her son's murderer. She couldn't stand to fuss over him anymore. Continuing with this playacting would amount to a betrayal.

"Don't worry, Thor, I'll avenge you."

How? There was no lack of possible methods: forget to draftproof the windows, serve him rotten food . . . The problem was that it was too obvious. She would easily be found out if they investigated. What to do, then?

Suddenly, she had a brilliant idea: a welcome-home party for his friends! Instead of avoiding contact, she only had to invite about twenty kids here and she'd have an army of killers.

Biological warfare! A banquet for microbes. Kids are the biggest carriers of diseases. Jonas would get some germ or virus that his immune system couldn't fight. That was it! A tragic anniversary! A homecoming party that turns sour! Nobody is guilty, or else everybody is . . . With Jonas's friends and their brothers and sisters, she would infect Jonas and the house.

She withdrew to her room to draw up a list.

How to carry out this plan before Katrin got back? She had to act quickly. Would it be possible to gather these human time bombs before April 16th? It was the 16th that Katrin was due back, wasn't it? She couldn't quite remember. It was already the 14th . . .

That night, Alba prepared her invitations, checked she had everyone's postal and e-mail addresses, and at last, exhausted, fell asleep as dawn broke.

*

On the morning of April 15th, Katrin left them a frantic message on the answering machine:

"Jonas, Alba, I won't be back tomorrow as planned. Switzerland is closing its airspace. Because of us, because of Eyjafjöll! Just my luck! You'll have to manage a bit longer without me. I don't know how long it's going to last. Love."

When they woke up, Alba and Jonas verified Katrin's information. The volcanic dust, pushed by the wind in a south-easterly direction, was converging on northern Europe. After some experts pointed out that dust particles could affect aircraft engines, the authorities of various countries had decided to close their air space. Britain and Poland had been the first, followed by Belgium, Switzerland, Norway, Denmark, and Ireland . . .

The aunt and the nephew reacted differently to this news.

Jonas felt a wave of nationalistic pride. "Do you realize, Auntie, a little country like ours is stopping international air traffic! Amazing, isn't it? It'll cost them millions and millions."

Alba, though, saw this event as a sign from fate: Katrin being stuck in Geneva gave her free rein to get rid of Jonas; she had to see her murderous plan through to the end.

She told her nephew that she had a big surprise for him, then shut herself in her room to phone the guests. She had planned the party for Thursday evening, the day after tomorrow. Within a day, she had received twenty positive replies.

On the Wednesday, as she was looking at the estimate from a caterer who specialized in birthdays, her cell phone rang.

"I found out!" Vilma cried at the other end of the line.

"What?"

"I found out what they did with my daughter."

"How?"

"Sturluson! At the Transplant Center. I went to see him, like you did, to try to get around him, but I didn't even need to meet with him. I overheard a conversation through the door. He was talking to a surgeon about an operation—an operation that took place the day my daughter died."

"You need more than that, Vilma."

"I know what I'm talking about."

With horror, Alba recognized herself in this statement.

"Join me at the usual place," Vilma ordered.

Confused, Alba stammered an explanation to Jonas, leapt into her car, and drove to Reykjavík.

When she entered the Mermaid Café, Vilma grabbed her arm. Alba looked down, and was reminded of a bird's claw encircling a branch.

"Help me."

"To do what?"

"To steal the child."

"What child?"

"The child who got my daughter's heart."

Aghast at this, Alba broke free. "I thought you only wanted to know."

"Oh, no! The only reason I've been doing this was to get my daughter back."

"'Get you daughter back?' Your daughter's dead, Vilma."

"No, you're wrong," Vilma moaned. "If my daughter's heart is throbbing somewhere, then she's still alive. If her heart is keeping a body alive, she'll recognize me. If her heart is beating, she needs me. She misses me, Alba, she's misses me, she's calling me, she needs to resume our life the way it was before." Vilma's eyes dimmed with tears. "If I delay any longer, she'll think I've abandoned her."

Vilma's crazy. Alba had only just realized where her friend's suffering had led her.

"Alba, please help me, we'll both go."

"I don't agree with it."

"Aren't you going to help me?"

"I'd really like to help you, but not to do something like that. You're not thinking straight, Vilma."

"Lend me your car."

"No."

"Fine, I'll go alone!"

Red-faced, feverish, resolute as a warrior, the frail Vilma stood up and ran to the door. Alba tried to stop her.

"Give this up, Vilma, it's madness! You're going to see a stranger, not your daughter."

"What do you know?"

With these words, Vilma ran out onto the street. By the time Alba had paid for their beers, the young woman had disappeared into the storm that was rising over the city.

Helpless, Alba hesitated. Of course, she had to do something. But what? Go to the police? It was too soon for that. Stop Vilma? She didn't even know where she lived.

She went back to the apartment and wrote to Erik the Red, the head of Liberaria. He quickly wrote back confirming that Vilma was deranged, but posing what he said was the real question—Who had made her like that?—and then launching into a relentless four-page diatribe against the Icelandic government.

Alba realized that she wouldn't get any help from that direction.

Magnus came in. For the first time in weeks, the sight of her husband delighted her, and she threw herself into his arms.

"Did you come back for me?" he asked.

"Of course."

By way of reward, he kissed her.

"I love you, Magnus, you know."

As she had foreseen, the results of these words were immediately confirmed in Magnus's jeans. Delighted that she could still have this effect on a man, she continued, whispering in his ear that she had missed him, that she couldn't bear being so far from him anymore. She even surprised herself with how well she was making all this up, and wondered if there wasn't some truth in her spontaneous invention.

Magnus lifted her in his arms, laid her down on the couch, and slowly undressed her with his big expert fingers.

They made love several times. They had all the time in the world, and no longer needed to hide: Thor wasn't there anymore, and Liv was looking after Jonas.

As she got dressed again, Alba remembered Vilma, and realized that sleeping with Magnus had distracted her. Should she tell Magnus about her? No, because then she would be forced to tell him about herself as well . . .

"Magnus, will you take me back to Katrin's house? You could stay with Jonas and me."

"How will I get to work tomorrow?"

"I'll drive you."

Magnus's enthusiastic agreement was marked with a kiss so moist and so prolonged that they almost made love again on the couch.

*

When they parked outside the house, they immediately noticed the signs that told them something was wrong. The outside lights were off—Jonas always left them on to help drivers to orientate themselves when there was a storm—and the interior seemed dark too. When they climbed the three steps that led to the door, they realized that it was banging in the wind. They hastened to enter.

Magnus went first, ready to attack the intruder . . . Nothing was moving inside the building. They called. No reply.

"That's impossible!" Alba said. "Jonas must be here."

They called again, then, without further ado, searched the rooms. No Jonas.

In the kitchen, they found Liv lying unconscious on the floor behind the counter.

Magnus revived her while Alba called the police and the emergency services.

Before the paramedics arrived, Liv regained consciousness and told them what had happened. "A woman rang the doorbell. I opened the door because I thought she'd gotten lost in the storm. She asked me if this was where Jonas lived. That surprised me. Then she told me she was one of the nurses that had taken care of him in the last few weeks and that she wanted to say hello to her favorite patient. I wasn't suspicious, she looked so kind, a little redheaded mouse . . . I took her to Jonas, and then, I don't know what happened . . . After being so lovely, she started scolding our boy. I went up to her and she punched me and knocked me out . . . My God! Jonas! Did she hit him too?"

"He isn't here," Magnus said.

"She took him with her," Alba said. "It's a kidnapping."

Magnus and Liv both turned to her, surprised by her certainty.

*

Until late into the night, Alba told the police officers what she knew, plus what she suspected. As far as she was concerned, there was no other possibility: the visitor could only have been Vilma.

Sitting not far from her, Magnus listened because it was partly for him that Alba was speaking.

Unfortunately, all she knew about Vilma was her cell phone number, which she had stopped answering, and which nobody could trace. To identify her, the police had to rely on the date of her daughter's death, which she had indicated was the same as that of Jonas's operation.

The results appeared on the computer. In Iceland that day there had only been two adolescents who could have provided organs: a certain Helga Vilmadottir and Thor Magnusson.

Alba bowed her head as if she had just been accused of a crime and was being taken to court. After a few seconds, she glanced at Magnus, who was just starting to grasp the whole thing: Alma's friendship with Vilma, her obsessive research, her distancing herself from him.

"Can they put a girl's heart in a boy?" a police officer asked in surprise. "The heart isn't a sexual organ," Magnus replied.

"There's no proof that Jonas received that heart," Alba said.

"Some people are really crazy!" the policeman concluded.

Alba stared at the tips of her pumps: Vilma wanted to capture Jonas to love him, Alba to kill him. How could she have thought like that? It suddenly struck her as stupid to claim that a body belonged to you, even more stupid to claim a right over a transplant patient. She had the feeling she was waking from a long nightmare.

But now a new nightmare had begun: Jonas's disappearance.

The police officers left. Alba and Magnus locked up the house and returned in silence to Reykjavík. They thought of the frail Jonas in the hands of a madwoman.

Once they were back in their apartment, Magnus grabbed two chairs and asked Alba to sit down facing him. She tried to kiss him, to cling to him, but he pushed her away.

"Stay where you are, Alba, and listen to me."

"But—"

"Let go of me, or I'll tie you to that chair."

She sat down, head bowed, like a little girl being punished.

"I'm going to tell you what I think, Alba, and you can tell me if I'm wrong. You're so ashamed of having left Thor after an argument in which you insulted him and threatened him like a harpy that you're running away from that memory. You want to avoid feeling guilty. So to protect yourself from remorse, your bad faith has led you to forget Thor, and you've been lashing out blindly, aiming at Jonas or at society the aggression you should have turned on yourself."

Alba started crying. "I wasn't a good mother!"

"Yes, you were, Alba. Not that night, because you couldn't control your nerves, but the other nights. Many nights. Thor was no angel. He wasn't as easy to love as Jonas. But you and I loved him and raised him as best we could." He kneeled down before her. "You resented Jonas for being alive. You fantasized God knows what, that Thor had been killed to save Jonas, some madness or other that suited you because it stopped you confronting your own sense of unease. You have to stop now, Alba, you can't think such nonsense anymore."

"I don't think it anymore."

"I know, because you're finally listening to me."

With a paternal gesture, he let her rest her head on his shoulder and breathe deeply.

"A little black death?"

She gave a start, forgetting for a moment that "black death" was the name given to *brennivin*, the national drink—aromatic brandy flavored with bergamot.

They both drank a glass, and then Magnus poured himself a second. "Now you're going to think and tell me as much as you can about Vilma. Maybe we can figure out where she's hiding Jonas."

*

Alba did not sleep a wink all night. In bed, sometimes lying on her left side, sometimes on her right, holding her breath in order not to wake Magnus, she tried to put herself in Vilma's shoes and couldn't manage it.

At seven in the morning, she called the police inspector who had given her his number, hoping that the professionals had been more effective than she had.

Embarrassed, the inspector told her that the investigation was certainly making progress but that they still had no idea where Vilma was keeping Jonas. They had discovered that she had no job and no family, and had had no fixed abode since her daughter's death.

Alba shuddered. Where was Jonas? Had he been bound and gagged to stop him escaping or calling out? If he went out into the cold of the storm, he wouldn't be able to withstand the violence of the elements . . .

She started walking up and down the apartment. Walking had always helped her to think. Each time, she stopped outside Thor's door, sighed, and set off again.

Suddenly, a detail drew her attention. Something was missing. She inspected the walls around her: the key to the cabin had disappeared.

"Magnus!"

She threw herself on her husband, woke him, and told him what she had deduced: Vilma must have taken refuge in their house in the mountains.

"How would she have got there? You told me she didn't have a car."

"She stole one. When you steal a child, you can steal a car, can't you? Magnus, she's taken Jonas to the most dangerous place in Iceland."

Angrily, he opened the closet and grabbed their mountain clothes.

"Let's get dressed and go!"

*

Around them, the ashes had cast a black pall over the landscape.

The volcanic cloud raced above their heads, organic and immense, driven by the winds that blew against the car. Swelling here, getting denser there, this plume drew terrifying figures: trumpets from the Day of Judgment, demons, bulls, trolls, chimera, an army of cruel and incredible monsters.

As the vehicle approached the eruption, the plume lost its shape, descended until it formed a dark ceiling that stifled the light. Then, as they came through a pass, this leaden ceiling reached the ground, becoming a black soup that turned the atmosphere opaque, reduced visibility, and blocked all movement.

At every moment, Alba and Magnus were afraid that they would be stopped by a roadblock. The area had become dangerous and had been forbidden to human activity. They shuddered at the thought of Jonas doomed to breathe this noxious air.

They glimpsed torches in the distance: the authorities were blocking off the perimeter of the explosion. Cautiously, Magnus stopped the car and switched out the lights, then set off along an adjacent path.

"How could Vilma have managed to get this far?" Alba asked, assailed by doubts.

"Don't forget she's with Jonas, and he knows the region like the back of his hand."

"He'd never tell her!"

"You don't know what people reveal under threat."

Alba swallowed her saliva. Jonas was in hell. As long as he had the strength . . .

Their car was rocking more and more, manhandled by the state of the road, which was not only covered with particles but strewn with stones.

Magnus braked abruptly. A sudden torrent had cut across the road, barring their way completely. It was impossible to go any further.

They put on hoods, as well as protective masks over their noses and mouths, then continued on foot.

An apocalyptic atmosphere reigned everywhere.

The wind wrapped itself around them, slowing their progress. It was coming down from the mountaintops, sharpening itself on the rocks, then charging on, as cutting as a steel blade.

When they reached the plateau where the cabin was, a gust of wind suddenly blew in the opposite direction and the view cleared. For a few seconds, the countryside was wrapped in a kind of lethargy, a lethargy that resembled a slow death, and they spotted a 4x4 parked five hundred yards from the house.

"They drove all the way here. They're inside, that's for sure!"

They would have liked to run but everything stopped them. Because it had been raining, the ash had stuck to the snow and become a lumpy glue that fixed the soles of their shoes to the ground, forcing them to make a huge effort with each step.

And in this flatter area, the wind tormented them in a different way, it was like a whiplash, stopping them from thinking. Its rumbling force seemed to be trying to kill all thought and sweep the surface of the earth.

At last they reached the cabin. Smoke was rising from the chimney, to be immediately dispersed by the wind.

Magnus signaled to Alba to keep quiet. He was relying on the effect of surprise.

With his shoulder, he shoved open the door.

Vilma, who was sitting next to Jonas, resting, had time only to see a body loom up in front of her before Magnus hit her on the head, stunned her, and tied her hands.

Once immobilized, Vilma blinked, realized what was happening, and started screaming.

Alba rushed to Jonas. His features were drawn, his nostrils contracted, and he was having difficulty breathing. She tapped his pale cheeks.

He opened his eyes and saw his aunt's face. "I knew you'd come . . . "

At these words, Vilma became even more vociferous. "Leave me alone. Don't touch her. She's my daughter. I recognized her in spite of everything. She didn't struggle, she's been nice to me, that's proof, isn't it?"

Magnus tried to gag her. She bit him and kicked him in the crotch. He grimaced. "What am I supposed to do with this maniac?"

Alba threw herself between them and looked Vilma up and down. "Tie her to the chair," she ordered Magnus. "I just want her to leave us in peace. We'll send the police to get her."

"Help me, Alba," Vilma moaned. "You agree with me, Alba. You're the only one."

"You're sick, Vilma, very sick, but I hope the doctors will help you get better."

"Take me with you."

Alba had to restrain herself from slapping her. "I don't trust you. Can't you see what a state you've put Jonas in? Because of you, he may die."

Magnus had rapidly dressed his nephew, put a mask on him, and without asking him for help, hoisted him on his shoulders. "Hang on tight, my boy, we're going!"

They left the cabin.

As soon as they were outside, the wind grew even stronger. Was such a long, sustained, relentless fit of temper possible?

The red house was still withstanding the assault but it was shaking, its joints creaked, and its roof quivered. From deep inside, they could hear Vilma's shrill sobs.

They staggered on, unable to concentrate. The wind was trying to empty their heads and the plain.

Suddenly, they heard an unusual noise. A kind of persistent rattle. Stones were falling.

"Cover yourselves, quickly!"

Alba was pointing to a rocky outcrop that she had always known, where she and Katrin had once planned some huts. They ran toward it. Around them, the volcanic fragments rained down, some as small as eggs, others as big as monoliths.

Jonas let out a cry. Alba and Magnus thought that he had been hit by a stone and turned in panic.

Jonas was pointing at the red cabin in the distance.

A huge stone had gone through the roof and smashed into the one room, and now the flames, released from the fireplace, were starting to lick the beams.

Within five minutes, the building was on fire. Then a gust of wind rushed across the plateau and buried it beneath the ashes.

*

Alba smiled. That diffuse light, that slight wind announced that something was about to be born: spring.

The sun was shining out of a calm sky. The seagulls were screaming with excitement. Soon, the earth would stop being as hard as stone, the grass would grow, the Alaska lupins would clothe the embankments in blue.

She was standing by the letterbox, waiting for Whistle.

The previous night, he had hacked into the hospital's computer system and printed out some documents.

There he was, coming up the path, swaying on his bicycle. You might wonder, seeing that figure, which was the thinner, he or the bicycle.

He approached Alba, brandishing the file victoriously. "Here it is!"

"How can I ever thank you?"

"By making the revolution, comrade. Let's not talk anymore, they may see us."

He left again immediately, freewheeling down the slope, getting smaller until he was just a dot on the road leading to Reykjavík.

With the envelope in her hand, Alba went back into the house, where Jonas was still asleep and Katrin was recovering from her tiring journey.

She took the sheets of paper from the folder, and without even glancing at them, fed them into the shredder. As the paper tore, she felt stronger, more passionate, more alive. Then she made some tea and toasted some bread.

There was a noise behind her.

Jonas appeared, blond, fresh, and as beautiful as the dawn in his coral-colored pajamas. "What a pity you canceled my homecoming party!" he said. "My friends were really looking forward to it."

Alba handed him his breakfast tray. "Later. It's only postponed. In the meantime, how about a little belote?"

THE GHOST CHILD

On the bench opposite mine, a woman was feeding the birds. Sparrows and blue tits had hopped timidly toward her, fearing to become earthbound again, ready to retreat back into the air at the slightest suspicious movement, then had come to rest at her feet, ever more numerous, drawn up in a semicircle like a chorus of beggars. Some of the bolder souls no longer hesitated to leap onto the bench, even onto the woman's thighs or arms. Attracted by the feast, a robin chased away its fellow creatures with stabs of its beak, and even clumsy pigeons waddled forward.

The picture intrigued me. It wasn't that I hadn't witnessed a scene like this a hundred times: a strange woman giving the birds a treat, regardless of those around her. But one thing was different today: this woman's appearance defied the cliché. She wasn't a bag lady, she wasn't poor or old, her strawberry blonde hair had only recently been tended to at the salon, she was wearing a stylish clear linen pantsuit, and her amber complexion was redolent of vacations by the sea or in the mountains, in other words the leisure of the well-to-do. An upper-middle-class lady was feeding the sparrows of Paris.

The friend I was with nudged me and whispered, "Look."

An individual of similar age and type—early sixties, sporty appearance—was walking along the path looking for a bench. On that first bright morning after long, dull weeks of rain, what Parisian wouldn't want to warm himself in the sun's rays? The walker noted that there was only one seat left, beside the bird lady.

Without a word of greeting, without even a glance, he sat down and behaved as if he were alone. He cleared his throat and opened wide his newspaper, encroaching on his neighbor's space.

The woman pretended not to notice him. For a moment, I thought she was throwing crumbs between the man's legs so that the noisy, aggressive birds would swarm around him.

A couple passed. The man looked up and greeted them. Three seconds later, the woman did the same. Then they each went back to their own activity, indifferent to the other. Having acquaintances in common did not seem to bring them together.

Suddenly, the wind blew one sheet of *Le Figaro* to the end of the bench. The woman did not move, as if nothing had happened, and let the man thrash about trying to catch it.

Later, in bending forward, she knocked over her bag, which rolled along the ground as far as the man's ankle. He reacted with indifference, merely crossing his legs.

Neither paid any attention to the other, and paradoxically you sensed that this was their main concern: not to pay attention to each other. Everything about them—the tension, the waves of scorn they emanated, the languid pace they imposed—suggested that they lived and breathed only to tell each other: *You aren't here.*

My friend was amused at my dismayed expression. "Would you believe they're husband and wife?"

"You're kidding."

"Not at all. They even live in the same house."

"They do?"

"But not together."

"Now I know you're talking nonsense . . . "

"They've cut their apartment in two. He comes and goes via the service entrance. They had a wall built so they never have to meet. Actually, they bump into each other twenty times a day, on the stairs, in the entrance hall, in the shops, on the street—especially as they've kept their old habits—but they ignore each other."

"You really are kidding me, aren't you?"

"If only you'd seen them a few years ago: they were so much in love. For the people in the neighborhood—around Place des Vosges, everyone knows everyone—they were the perfect couple, a model of harmony, the paradigm of a happy marriage! Who would have thought?"

"What happened?"

"One morning, they divided their property—the apartment, the chalet in the mountains, the house by the sea—and they haven't talked to each other since. It happened suddenly."

"Impossible . . . "

"If people can fall in love at first sight, why can't they fall out of love in the same way?"

"I wish I could understand."

"You're lucky, then! I learned the truth from a friend of Séverine's."

"Who's Séverine?"

"The bird lady opposite you."

*

Séverine and Benjamin Trouzac collected the signs of success: they were good-looking, young, popular, and their careers had prospered.

A graduate of the National Business School, Benjamin Trouzac worked at the Ministry of Health, where he dealt with the most difficult assignments. He was highly regarded for his sharp intelligence, his natural authority, his in-depth knowledge of cases, his strong sense of the public good.

Séverine was a freelance journalist who wrote lively, amusing articles for several women's magazines. Capable of knocking off a humorous column about making muffins or ten hilarious pages on the latest colors of nail polish, she delighted editors with her mixture of intelligence and frivolity.

The only thing missing was children. They both wanted a family, but kept putting it off. They liked to enjoy themselves too much, loved going out, loved friends, travel, sports.

When Séverine turned thirty-five, she became alarmed at how quickly time was passing. The moment had come, they decided, to start a family.

At this time, Séverine's sister gave birth to a daughter who had a rare disease.

Séverine was shattered for her sister, but Benjamin was horrified for the two of them. "I'm afraid of what's in store for us. Believe it or not, there are there are handicapped children in my family too. These things are no joke, Séverine!"

Séverine put off having a test for as long as possible, but her longing to be a mother had become so urgent that she eventually yielded to Benjamin's entreaties. The specialist they consulted—a female doctor friend of Benjamin's, whom he had met at the Ministry—did not beat about the bush: she told them that they were bearers of genes that exposed their offspring to disabilities.

"So what do we do?" Séverine asked.

"Well, when you become pregnant, we'll take samples, and then you can make an informed decision."

Séverine and Benjamin sighed with relief. Disconcerted as they were to know the truth, they realized that even though there was a risk they could continue with their plans.

The year Séverine turned thirty-seven, after several false alarms, she at last became pregnant.

Séverine and Benjamin were so overjoyed they almost forgot the advice they had been given. Luckily, Benjamin ran into his doctor friend at an international conference, and she reminded him of what he had to do.

One gray Monday, at eight in the morning, in the bare office of a run-down hospital, a consultant in genetics informed Séverine, who was smugly holding her round belly in her hands, that her fetus had a dangerous disease, cystic fibrosis, an ailment in which mucus accumulates in the respiratory and digestive tracts. Being as honest as he could be, he told the couple that the child would suffer from pulmonary problems, that it would require a great deal of care and treatment, and that its life expectancy would be limited. For these reasons, he informed Séverine, she would be given the right to abort even though her pregnancy was quite advanced.

Séverine and Benjamin faced a week of torment, torn between the desire to keep the baby and not to keep it. Depending on their mood, they either felt quite capable of bringing up a child who was different or were overwhelmed at the prospect. Their friends from the Ministry of Health provided them with conflicting opinions: according to some their child wouldn't live beyond the age of fourteen, while according to others it could survive to forty-five. Who to believe? The doctors they consulted were equally contradictory. One evening, placing themselves in the hands of fate, they threw dice, but as soon as the game gave them an answer, they rejected it in horror and refused to trust their future to chance. In short, after a week of inner conflict, they still had not chosen.

It was a TV program that helped them make up their minds. Channel hopping, they came across a report on the care of severely sick children. The presenter of the program had a political ax to grind—he wanted the government to commit itself to providing more care for the handicapped—and so painted a deliberately bleak picture, showing the daily lives of the patients and their parents in a tragic light. Séverine and Benjamin were so shocked and appalled at the thought of the ordeal that not only awaited them, but which they would inflict on the as-yet-unborn child, that they agreed to terminate the pregnancy. They contacted the hospital.

The weeks that followed the operation almost put an end to their marriage.

The reproaches came thick and fast, constant, sharp, and aggressive, addressed more to themselves than to each other. She blamed herself for being the carrier of the gene and urged him to leave her, while he complained of having held back her desire to be a mother for too long and encouraged her to regain her independence. They each considered themselves unhappy and misunderstood. The grief that should have brought them together isolated them from one another. Since they never spoke of the child they had turned into a ghost, Séverine felt that Benjamin downplayed her pain as a woman and Benjamin was sorry that Séverine ignored his grief as a man. Discreetly, they began cheating on each other. They did it often but sadly, without any real appetite or taste for it, and with a kind of desperate determination that drove them to sleep with strangers the way one might throws oneself into a river: "If the current carries me away, fine; if not, I'll swim to the bank."

Then they found a therapy that saved their marriage.

Séverine and Benjamin began again to live with all the carefree abandon of their first years together. They traveled, doted on their friends, and practiced their favorite sports. They couldn't be parents, so they became lovers again, and above all partners.

"My marriage is my child," Séverine would say, a smile on her lips, whenever her acquaintances commented in amazement on the understanding between them.

Since it had turned out there was no way for them to have children, their duo became an end in itself.

In the course of a day, they would smile at each other a thousand times, as if they had just met. After twenty years of living together, Benjamin bought as many roses as a young lover, while Séverine would run to the shops to buy clothes to surprise and seduce her man. They put such energy, refinement, and inventiveness into their lovemaking that sex remained an exciting adventure.

"My marriage is my child." Their relationship had become a collaboration, the object of constant attention, kept alive by their ingenuity.

They would have maintained this defiant attitude until the day they died, inventing a new version of Tristan and Isolde that would last for all eternity, if that accident had not happened in Chamonix . . .

*

Could they ever have imagined that the Alps would become their tomb? For these two winter sports fanatics, the mountains had always been a source of deep pleasure, giving them dazzling light, intoxicating speed, and the euphoria of achievement. Where some people relieved their childhood memories beside the sea, Séverine and Benjamin rediscovered their youth whenever they came to a mountain pass. Walking, climbing, skiing—they didn't care how they got across the mountains, every way was a delight. Until they made one expedition too many . . .

Very early that morning, they caught the cable car to the top of the Aiguille du Midi.

Both being highly skilled skiers, they decided to leave the well-marked *pistes*, which were as crowded as the streets of Paris, in order to enjoy the mountains in solitude.

The Alps stretched before them, both smooth and jagged, peaks and ridges alternating with plateaus and belvederes.

What a privilege! The snow was immaculate, untouched. Everything around them was pure, including the silence. They had the impression that they had been reborn beneath that cloudless sky, in that clean, healthy air, burned by the harsh sun.

Far from the dark valley below, the summits offered up their spotless surfaces.

Séverine and Benjamin glided along, weaving as lightly and smoothly as if they were swimming. The atmosphere was becoming liquid, granting them the intoxication of moving gracefully, freely, harmoniously, filled with a joy as fierce as the rays of the sun.

They sped across the heavy but diaphanous snow. Here and there, the white ground glittered like diamonds.

Suddenly Benjamin, who was in front, let out a cry. Séverine had just enough time to bend, then she, too, screamed.

The ground gave way beneath them, they hung in the air for a fraction of a second, then fell for what seemed an interminable time, grazing themselves on the sides, unable to grab on to anything.

At last they crashed onto an icy floor.

A few moments later, dazed, wild-eyed, devoid of their sticks and their skis, which had scattered during the fall, they came to their senses and realized they had fallen into a crevasse.

Another kind of peace reigned here, muffled and disturbing. All birdsong had ceased. Not a noise, not a sound. All life seemed extinguished.

"Are you in one piece, Séverine?"

"Yes, I think so. How about you?"

"I think I am, too."

Knowing that they were not injured was no real comfort. The problem remained: How to get out?

How far were they from the surface? At least forty or fifty feet . . . Impossible to get back up without help.

They shouted.

In turn, they looked up at the narrow slit of sky above them and yelled. Salvation could come only from that line, beyond the fatal walls that had swallowed them.

Their mouths were burning, thirst laid waste to their throats, their limbs grew rigid. Since their fall, a damp cold had penetrated their layers of clothing, sliding down their necks, insinuating itself between their sleeves and their gloves, turning their socks stiff, and flooding their shoes.

At regular intervals, they shouted.

During these calls for help, the noise they emitted gave them energy, and they urged themselves on to produce an infernal racket, each covering the other's voice.

All to no avail . . .

Nobody heard them.

And for good reason . . . they had ventured so far from the *pistes*, across the pearly, powdery snow, that they had distanced themselves from any well-frequented path. To hear their screams, some reckless soul would have to chance by, and that was extremely unlikely.

After a few hours, exhausted, they no longer had the desire to yell: they hated the roller coaster of emotions it created in them, the way their hopes were shattered every time by the lack of response . . .

They looked at each other, their jaws trembling, their skin puffed and raw.

"We're going to die," Séverine murmured.

Benjamin nodded sadly. It was pointless hiding the truth from each other.

Séverine lowered her eyes and let the hot tears run down over her cheeks. Benjamin took hold of Séverine's gloved hands and forced her to look at him.

"Séverine, you are the love of my life. I was lucky to meet you, to get to know you, and to be loved by you. Those are the only good memories I will take away with me from my time on earth."

She looked back at him, her eyes wide, and said in a numb voice, "I don't have any other good memories to take away with me either."

Tearing himself away from the ice, Benjamin came closer to her. She collapsed in his arms. They kissed fiercely.

Then they broke free and, with renewed vigor, started yelling again. They shouted themselves hoarse. They had no illusions, but they had to play their roles to the end. It was a duty.

The tomb of snow and ice that had walled them up remained silent. The only thing that changed was the light. It was turning gray as color drained from the sky. It would soon be dark . . .

They shivered at the thought of the night they would have to endure.

"Hello? Hello? Is there someone down there?"

They gave a start.

A head had appeared above them, in the slit: a young girl with a thin, energetic face. Their hearts went wild, and they screamed.

"I'll go for help," she cried in a clear voice.

"You won't have time to go down to the valley and come up again. It'll be night soon. Send us down a rope."

"I'm skiing, I don't have a rope."

Séverine and Benjamin looked at each other in dismay. Their hope had just been dashed.

Up above, the face vanished.

Benjamin jumped and hit the wall. "Don't go! Please stay!" he screamed, almost demented with panic. Unable to move, Séverine stared at him without reacting.

Then the silence fell again, sharp, dense, oppressive. Neither dared ask what the other was thinking. They were shivering with cold.

Time slipped away. One minute. Ten minutes. Half an hour. An hour. She wasn't coming back.

"Catch!" the girl called to them from up above, and began threading an orange rope through the slit. Cleverly, she had gone to the nearest *piste* and grabbed the rope joining the posts that lined the sides. Now she had tied it firmly to a rock and was lowering it toward the trapped couple.

Séverine grabbed hold of it first, summoned her last remaining strength and, ten minutes later, extricated herself from the hole. Then, in turn, Benjamin performed the same maneuver.

Back on the surface, sitting on the snow, suffering from chills and bruises, they peered through the fading light at their liberator: Mélissa, twenty years old. She was roaring with laughter. For her, this rescue had been a tremendous adventure.

*

At the chalet, Séverine and Benjamin warmed themselves, tended to their wounds, consulted a doctor, coated themselves with the prescribed ointments, gulped down painkillers and anti-inflammatories, then telephoned Mélissa. They did not want to leave without thanking her again.

Without any self-consciousness, she invited them to a party she was throwing with some friends.

Séverine and Benjamin celebrated their return to life surrounded by some fifteen lively young people between the ages of eighteen and twenty-two. They had all known each other since childhood, and often spent their vacations together.

Warmed by the wine, the jokes, and the jovial atmosphere in the restaurant, Séverine and Benjamin gazed lovingly at their benefactress. Dancing wildly to a rock number, Mélissa seemed to them to possess all the qualities wrapped up in one person: strength, intelligence, vivacity, kindness, energy.

One of the young men, seeing them looking at her, sat down next to them. "Mélissa's great, isn't she?"

"Oh, yes!" Séverine exclaimed.

"She really is," the young man murmured. "And to think she's seriously ill . . . Nobody would ever guess it."

"I beg your pardon?"

"Yes. Mélissa has cystic fibrosis. Didn't you know?"

Séverine and Benjamin turned white. Silent, mouths open, hands shaking, they sat pinned to their seats, their eyes riveted on Mélissa. They had just seen a ghost.

A WRITER'S DIARY

AUTHOR'S NOTE

Having gotten into the habit, in the second editions of my books, of adding a writer's diary, I have discovered that readers like it, so now I sometimes add these pages to the first edition. These are passages from my diary concerning my work in progress.

A friend of mine, one of the best theatrical makeup artists around, who lives with a psychiatrist, tells me how they became partners. Several decades ago, the two men got married in the darkness at the back of a church, hidden by pillars, while up at the altar, flooded with light, a wedding ceremony was taking place.

I find the anecdote a touching one. Humor is so rare in love, and so is humility! Personally, I think of these unpretentious lovers who wanted to be united before God as being very Christian.

Their act shows the strength of a passion that ignores taboos, defies appearances, and obtains what it is not entitled to.

This "pretend" marriage has lasted for more than thirty years . . .

"What about the 'proper' marriage?" I ask my friend. "How did that work out?"

He doesn't know.

I can't help but ponder. Did the couple that officially swore "to have and to hold" keep their vows? Has the legitimate love, encouraged by society, lasted as long as the illegitimate one?

*

I think again about my friends, the clandestine couple. Maybe it's because society has marginalized them that they've been able to give new meaning to the vows they swore in an echo of the official couple.

Their fidelity doesn't involve castrating or shackling each other. It is positive, committed to always giving the other person what you have promised—love, help, care and support—but not restrictive. For these two friends, who have allowed each other to have affairs, you don't have to lock your partner up in a cage in order to be a couple.

I seem to be back with Diderot, the hero of my play *The Libertine*. However, I am absolutely convinced that this liberal fidelity is easier to realize in same-sex couples because, in order to understand the other person you only have to examine yourself, whereas between a man and a woman there is a need to come to grips with the unknown.

Whereas infidelity is a tragedy in a male-female couple, one that may end in a breakup, an all-male couple is less worried about the impulses that lead to fleeting affairs. Whether or not they give in to those impulses, they acknowledge them, because they instinctively know what male sexuality is. What gives such a relationship an insolent ease is that the other person is the same as you, whereas between a man and a woman the other person remains another person. Sincerity and clearheadedness are not enough, it takes a long apprenticeship, not only to understand the opposite sex, but to actually get along with it.

*

During a train journey from Paris to Brussels, I scribbled a story called "Two Gentlemen from Brussels" in my notebook. At the Gare du Nord in Paris it was still very vague. By the time I got to the Gare du Midi in Brussels, an hour and twenty minutes later, this vague thing, like molten metal turning into a solid object, had taken on the shape and density of a story with a beginning, a middle and an end, characters and various episodes that had grown organically. Will I ever be able to repay my debt to the railroad companies? So many of my books have been conceived and hatched while I was being shaken about in a train . . .

It all starts with an image: two men unite in secret during a wedding ceremony. At first, the two couples—one glowing before the altar, the other hidden in the darkness of the back row—are brought together by sheer chance, but the clandestine couple will keep an eye out for the official couple.

This story has given me the chance to explore the differences between a homosexual and a heterosexual couple, the joys and sorrows specific to each, some of them diametrically opposed. Having completed my first draft, I have realized, somewhat to my surprise, that the happier of the two couples was perhaps not the one sanctioned by society and fêted in the church square.

When a man and a woman are joined in matrimony, they are under intense external pressure: their conjugal life is both encouraged and imposed, there are models to follow, a philosophy to be obeyed. But when two men set up home together, they are venturing on a terrain with few signposts, especially as society often rejects their union, or, when it does tolerate it, expects nothing of it. There is a paradoxical freedom in living a life that is either forbidden or scorned.

*

Is this a purely homosexual form of suffering?

A love that, however strong, however great, however long-lasting, does not produce a child . . .

Of course, infertility doesn't affect only homosexuals—there are heterosexuals who cannot have children—but it does affect all homosexuals.

*

I have finished writing " Two Gentlemen from Brussels."
I'm not sure how to classify this story. Is it a novella or a
long short story?

*

Some encouraging reactions from those who read it. "Two
Gentlemen from Brussels" touches people who have very different attitudes.

I'm pleased, but the question remains: what to do with the
story?

Publish it as it is or wait until there are other stories I can
combine it with? But which ones and why?

*

For once, I have asked myself a question that has an answer.

The two men I wrote about in "Two Gentlemen from
Brussels" have cousins, and they have introduced them to
me . . . Other stories have appeared, linked by a similar
theme: invisible loves.

*

One story conceals another. If you catch the first one, you
have a good chance of spotting those that follow.

A book of short stories is a series of game animals hunted
in a particular territory. Although the stories may vary, they
also have a lot in common.

If they didn't, putting them together would be an arbitrary
business. I think of my books of short stories not as collections
or anthologies, but as works composed organically. So I am

going to give the stories that will eventually make up this volume the overall title *Invisible Love*.

*

What has intrigued me in writing the title story is the idea of oblique feelings: feelings we don't admit either to ourselves or to our nearest and dearest, feelings that, although they are present in us, although they may stir us to action, are nevertheless located on the edges of our consciousness. In the title story, for example, Jean and Laurent experience virtual femininity through their fascination with Geneviève, then virtual fatherhood through keeping an eye on young David.

Their lives are based on an underlying architecture of feelings, one that is not formulated, one that is immaterial, but that nevertheless gives structure and support to the whole edifice. Many of our aspirations and desires are fulfilled symbolically.

*

We all live two lives—one real, the other imaginary.

And these two lives are like Siamese twins, more closely interlinked than we might think, because the parallel world often reshapes reality and even changes it.

This will be the theme of this new book of short stories: virtual lives that lie in the background of a real life.

* * *

I write the next story in the volume, "The Dog," with genuine passion. It has two sources: my personal life and some reflections I had, when I was a doctoral student at the École

Normale in the 1980s, on reading the work of the philosopher Emmanuel Lévinas.

My personal life: I have always lived with animals and I hope to enjoy their company until the day I die. For some years now, three Shiba Inu dogs have been my writing companions—at this very moment, the male is lying by my feet under the desk, while the two females are sprawled nearby—one on the rug and the other one on her bed. My music companions too, since they come running whenever I play the piano, get under the instrument to feel the vibrations, and listen to Chopin, not just with their ears, but with their whole bodies. They are also my companions during walks and games . . . When I talk to them, I talk to souls that have intelligence, sensitivity, feelings, and memory. Far from using them as toys, I treat them like people—people I cherish and who adore me. Even though some regard my attitude with disapproval, I am constantly trying to make them happy. Didn't I say I love them?

My intellectual life: At the age of twenty, I was struck by an essay about animals by Emmanuel Lévinas called "Nom d'un chien," published in his collection *Difficile liberté*. In it he recounts how, while a prisoner in a Nazi labor camp, he was paid a visit by a stray dog. The exuberant animal did not look askance at Jews as inferior beings or "subhumans," but would wag its tail at them as though they were normal men. "The last Kantian in Nazi Germany, without the brains necessary to universalize the maxims of his instincts," this dog gave him back his lost humanity.

This essay is all the more surprising in that it virtually contradicts his philosophy.

It is Emmanuel Lévinas's contention that the basic experience of humanity is that of the face. A human face looks at another human face and enters into an intersubjective relationship. In it, he sees not eyes, but a look, because "the best way to meet another person is not even to notice the color of his eyes! When you notice the color of his eyes, you are not in a social relationship with the other person." At that moment he recognizes in the other person a person who is not him, he sees a fellow human being, someone worthy of respect, someone who must not be put to death. I shudder at the idea that the experience of a face is an ethical experience. "The face is that which you cannot kill, or at least whose meaning is 'Thou shalt not kill.' Murder, admittedly, is an everyday event: one can kill someone else; ethical standards are not an ontological necessity. The taboo against killing does not make murder impossible, although the authority of the taboo is maintained in the guilty conscience engendered by the committing of an evil deed—the malignity of evil." (*Ethics and Infinity*). The Nazis stopped at this experience of the face when they considered Jews, Gypsies, homosexuals, and cripples as being on the level of inferior animals. Yet, "'Thou shalt not kill' is the first word of the face. And it is an order. In the appearance of the face there is a commandment, as if a master were speaking."

The strangeness of barbarism. It eludes lived experience. It blinds itself.

A dog, though, is incapable of it.

Does that make it more human than human beings? It is certainly not racist. And it is never perverted by ideology.

But why does a dog see a face that the executioners cannot see? And does a dog have a face?

When he was asked this, Lévinas evaded the question. His experience as a prisoner fêted by a stray dog remained marginal to his thought.

My lecturer at the École Normale, the philosopher Jacques Derrida, dared to go further in one of his last essays, in which he recounts how his cat saw him naked and he suddenly felt ashamed. Someday I'll come back to that . . .

*

The end of the story "The Dog" is about forgiveness.

Forgiveness?

Nothing strikes me as more difficult.

Here, my protagonist, Dr. Samuel Heymann, manages, thanks to his dog, to grasp the humanity that still exists in the traitor and turn his back on revenge. I admire his strength, which reminds me of a real person I have been much concerned with in the past few years: Otto, the father of Anne Frank.

Currently, at the Théâtre Rive-Gauche, under the direction of Steve Suissa, a company of actors, including Francis Huster, is rehearsing the play I wrote based on *The Diary of Anne Frank*. Thanks to the historians of the Anne Frank House in Amsterdam and the members of the Anne Frank Foundation in Basel, I discovered that Otto Frank never did anything to encourage an investigation into who gave him and his family and his friends away when they were hiding in the annex. In my play, when another character is outraged by the fact that a bastard can sleep peacefully after sending eight people to their deaths, Otto goes so far as to say, "I pity his children."

Otto Frank did not want to add violence to violence. He saw a certain kind of justice not as fairness, but as revenge. That is really sublime.

Too much so?

I don't know. If someone attacks my family, I'm quite capable of murder.

I'm not worthy of my own characters.

*

I have finished "The Dog" in a state of great emotion. Although I started out thinking that Samuel Heymann was very different from me—apart from the gratitude he feels toward his dogs—I wonder if he doesn't carry within him my own latent misanthropy, the misanthropy I try to suppress.

Let us be clear about this: I'm known to be inquisitive and cheerful, I love mankind in all its complexity, I enjoy meeting new people, I'm passionate about both individuals and books—otherwise I wouldn't be a novelist, a playwright, or a reader—yet my faith in human beings has its ups and downs. It doesn't happen often, but it does happen with some regularity, that I have to use all my willpower to remember that I love the human race even though its violence, its injustice, its stupidity, its shilly-shallying, its indifference to beauty, and above all its acceptance of mediocrity shock me.

One must love mankind . . . but how hard mankind is to love! Just as one cannot be an optimist without knowing pessimism intimately, one cannot love mankind without hating it a little. A feeling always carries its opposite. It's up to each of us to choose the right one.

* * *

What joy! Here I am, rubbing shoulders with Mozart again. I suppose he is the most important man in my life—I'm talking here of the dead—a man who provokes a sense of wonder, an appreciation of beauty, joy, and energy, a man who leads me to an awed approval of mystery.

This time, I'm not giving him French words, as I did with *The Marriage of Figaro* and *Don Giovanni*, or recounting *My Life with Mozart*, but writing a story in which he is a constant but invisible presence.

I am astonished by the speed with which, after his death, Mozart moves from obscurity into the limelight. A man who wears himself out in his desperate search for money, commissions, recognition, a man who is buried at the age of thirty-five in a common grave with nobody attending the funeral, but who, within two decades, is considered the symbol of musical genius throughout Europe, raised to the heights of fame, where he has remained ever since.

What happened?

Mozart was an eighteenth-century composer whose true career was in the nineteenth century. Even though he died in 1791, he was the first nineteenth-century composer, the embodiment of the new artist. Picked out and loved by other composers—such as Haydn, who said of him that he was "the greatest composer known to me either in person or by name"—he enjoyed a particular aura during the Romantic era because those who came after him, first Beethoven, Rossini, and Weber, then Chopin, Mendelssohn, Liszt, and Berlioz, became independent creators. Fulfilling Mozart's wish, they freed themselves from those in power and took the arbitration of taste away from kings, princes and aristocrats: it was they who now dictated what was good and bad in music. Mozart became their composer, a composers' composer. Then he was adopted by the people and became everyone's composer.

His widow, Constanze Mozart, née Weber, and Baron Nissen, her second husband, played an important role in this process, since during those years they catalogued his works and had them published and performed.

Historians disagree on who was the more influential of the two. Most, taking their cue from Mozart's father and sister, see Constanze merely as a charming but scatterbrained woman, incapable of acting responsibly, practically, or consistently. Some recent biographers of Constanze, though, have tried to rehabilitate her by highlighting the work she did for Mozart after his death.

The more we look into the question, the more we realize what a significant role Baron Nissen played. He did not just help Constanze: this Danish diplomat, at once meticulous, passionate, and opinionated, sorted through the scores, wrote to publishers, and negotiated contracts on her behalf; he even obtained Constance's signature in order to manage everything concerning Mozart; last but not least, bringing together records and eyewitness accounts, he undertook, of his own accord, to write a major biography of Mozart. And it is in this book that he rehabilitates Constanze, his wife, as Mozart's wife—in opposition to the slanderous assertions of Mozart's sister Nannerl. His defense of Constanze is both logical and strange. Logical because he lives with her. Strange because he lives with his rival's ghost.

It is tempting to find this situation amusing, as Antoine Blondin did, or to look for some hidden explanation—repressed homosexuality, according to Jacques Tournier in *Le Dernier des Mozart*. In my case, what fascinates me is the mystery of how a man can be so passionate about another man who was his wife's first husband.

I can only see this household as a *ménage à trois*.

*

Why should there be a hidden explanation—and why only one—for Nissen's attitude toward Mozart? Why should this passion he feels for his wife's first husband have just one dimension: a devotion to genius, homosexual leanings, financial interest, a love triangle, an exploration of his femininity?

What if it was all of these things at the same time?

Literature warns us against simple ideas. In this respect, it is very different than ideology, which tends to seek the elementary beneath plurality.

Ideologists, eager to reduce the multiplicity of appearances to an easily located principle, stop questioning their implicit prejudice: that truth is simple.

But why?

Why shouldn't truth be complex and made up of many causes?

Why should the fantasy of the elementary win the day?

The ideal of simplicity is illuminating at first, but then it blinds us.

As advocates of complexity, novelists discover connections, pushing their investigation as far as it will go, whereas ideologists search in this same diversity to find a foundation.

Ideologists dig, novelists illuminate.

*

Moralists never make good novelists. When they try, they bring to their reproduction of reality a coldness, a clinical attitude, a dissection of living matter that reeks of the laboratory.

Instead of taking us to a maternity ward, they trap us in a morgue.

That may be interesting, but it's never attractive.

Unless one appreciates the poetry of a forensic pathologist . . .

* * *

A journey to Iceland with my mother. The liner slices through the waves, taking us to the land of perpetual daylight.

In this infinity of water and sky, we think about Father, who left us two weeks ago.

We talk about him calmly, tenderly, joyfully, as if he could still hear us.

This cruise was arranged long before he lay dying, but his death was very predictable, coming as it did after years of suffering, and I knew we would make this journey while mourning him.

He himself suspected as much, he hoped it would happen, talked to me about it, entrusted my mother to me for when he was gone. We are happy to grant his wish.

There is a bright, clear, peaceful atmosphere to this journey: is it the light of destiny fulfilled?

*

I have a short story in my head, one about a transplanted heart, and I decide to set it in Iceland.

I love this country. This is the third time I've been here. Whether in winter or in summer—I think there are only two seasons—I am overwhelmed by that rough volcanic crust rising from the sea. Nature here is not just the flora or fauna, it is the earth, inhabited by violent, dangerous forces, lava capable of tearing open rocks and glaciers. It slumbers, vibrates, boils, cracks, explodes. If you want to experience a land that is alive, even when you can't see plants or animals, go to Iceland.

In this country of basalt and ashes, human beings are a spicy blend of sweet and sour. Crushed as they are by the forces of nature, they demonstrate great humility and solidarity. Was it not here that the world's first parliament assembled in the ninth century?

"A Heart Under Ash" tells the story of a woman who loves her nephew more than her son, developing maternal feelings not for her own child but for her sister's. When her son dies in an accident, she suddenly realizes this and, in order to expiate—or escape—her guilt, she is forced to hate her nephew. Her previous love for him is replaced by an equally strong hate.

Impulsive, accustomed to expressing herself with a paintbrush rather than in words, she is incapable of formulating her emotions and unsuited to introspection. It is better for her not to put her thoughts and attitudes into sentences because, whenever she tries, she gets it wrong. Her husband, for example, into whose arms she throws herself without hesitation, she speaks of with contempt; she describes her beloved sister as a tyrant; she thinks her new friend Vilma is an angel whereas in fact she conceals a devil; as for her son, he was nothing but a list of complaints . . .

If words fail some people, Alba uses them to betray herself.

That means that my story, which is told from Alba's point of view, cannot resort to psychological analysis. It must keep to the facts. It must describe the action as if in a film. Sometimes I have the feeling I'm writing it not with a pen, but with a camera.

*

Vilma is Alba's double. These two mothers have their grief in common; like many people nowadays, they cannot bear moral pain.

Our preposterous era rejects suffering. After centuries of Christianity, whose emblem is a dying man nailed to a pair of wooden planks, our materialistic world has a tendency to flee Calvary. When we feel sad, we swallow medication, we take drugs, we see a therapist.

As for Vilma and Alba, they act to suppress their affliction.

This desire not to feel anymore will lead them to become monsters. One hopes to steal Jonas, the other to kill him. They kidnap or murder because they do not want to confront their own sense of unease.

To act . . . I have often thought that strong, enterprising, dynamic men who kill themselves when they're about forty or fifty are also men who, accustomed to controlling their own lives, evade suffering with an act—the act of hanging themselves or blowing their brains out.

Suicide out of a desire to act rather than the lessening of desire.
Suicide because of a misunderstanding.
Suicide because they are incapable of facing their own pain.
All wisdom starts with the acceptance of suffering.

*

In "A Heart Under Ash" I ask the question: What is a person?
Is a part of a person still him? Is my heart, my kidney, my liver still me?
In transplant surgery, organs are regarded as almost interchangeable biological spare parts: when brain death makes a human being lose his overall feeling, he is reduced to a warehouse of these spare parts.
The ego is therefore the living, synchronous totality of the body. All that remains afterwards are the scattered elements that once formed the whole.
Vilma, one of my two heroines, rejects this viewpoint. She regards her daughter's heart as her daughter.
Alba, on the other hand, thinks Thor was destroyed when they removed his heart.
In a way, both challenge death. Vilma denies it, and Alba wants to believe that it could have been avoided.

*

As a supporter of organ donation, I like the idea that death can be useful.

*

Death is nothing but a service rendered to life so that it can be renewed and continue.
If the earth were filled with immortals, how would we coex-

ist? We would need to find a way to make room for new generations.

Death is the wisdom of life.

*

If Romanticism is all about the harmony between nature and human beings, then "A Heart Under Ash" is a Romantic story. The forces of the earth get angry and are unleashed at the same time as my protagonists, then calm down in unison with their hearts.

* * *

I am writing the last story in the book, "The Ghost Child." Or, rather, I am rewriting it, since I already wrote a version of it a few months ago.

That was an unpleasant episode. A newspaper I like very much asked me for a Christmas story. In response, I sent them this story. How embarrassing for them—and then for me. What I had delivered wasn't what they wanted at all. "The Ghost Child" was rather a harsh, uncompromising story, completely lacking in the magical, warmhearted, playful tone required of "a Christmas story."

The editor's stammered apology over the phone took me completely aback. It had never even occurred to me that something I wrote had to meet seasonal criteria. Once again, I was discovering that I was incapable of practicing journalism and unsuited to working on commission.

The editor had the good grace to search in some of my previous books for a short story that was better suited to "the spirit of Christmas."

"The Ghost Child" is inspired by my close friends. Out of respect and love for them, I wish both to point that out and to keep silent.

What parent hasn't dreaded the announcement: "Your child will not be normal"? We know some who have embraced this fate, and others who have rejected it. While I praise those who have welcomed a handicapped child, I would never cast a stone at those who have preferred abortion. Often, in fact, it is the same people. I know parents who are raising their sick children alongside other, healthy, ones, while haunted by the ghosts of one or more rejected children.

And I think I know how a friend of mine must feel when he looks at his daughter—lively, pretty, intelligent, and optimistic, although suffering from a rare condition—and thinks of her virtual brothers and sisters that he and his wife once chose not to allow to be born. When he thrills with joy and love for his daughter, he must miss them. When he takes her to hospital for her treatment and worries about new infections, he has to justify that rejection. I am sure he constantly wavers between one and the other, and that this wavering gives him a human depth and density that we admire in him.

*

Some time ago, I read a scientific article that proved that Chopin did not have tuberculosis, as was thought at the time, but a form of cystic fibrosis, a rare lung disease that had not yet been identified.

It made my head swim.

Knowing that these days reliable genetic tests can detect a great number of illnesses either prior to conception or during pregnancy, I imagined Mr. and Mrs. Chopin being summoned to the hospital and told about their son's breathing difficulties, his reduced life expectancy, the problems he and they would have to face day by day. Maybe the doctor would even make them feel guilty by telling them they would be costing society a lot of money if they let this child be born.

Then Mr. and Mrs. Chopin would give up on little Frédéric, and mankind would be deprived of all that wonderful music that soothes us in our solitude.

*

Without bringing in that old word "eugenics," a frightening word that evokes the horrors of the Nazi period, we are moving toward practices that are increasingly unquestioned.

Today, an accountant's mentality is emerging in the field of life. We calculate what this or that illness will cost society. We quibble over access to certain medicines that could give a sick person just a few more months of life, and we reject effective treatments that are too expensive.

In fact, some civil servants have already decided how much a life is worth. The pragmatic British have created NICE—the National Institute for Clinical Excellence—a highly positioned health authority defining the sum that society agrees to pay in treatment and medication for each year of life extended. Take your calculators: it's £40,000 a year. If new treatments exceed this price, Social Security, relying on advice from NICE, refuses to reimburse the cost. This accountant's mentality has spread to Austria and Sweden. Obviously, the various government debt crises are encouraging this development.

Well, not everything that is rational is reasonable.

The economic rationale is no longer reasonable if it attacks human beings, their dignity, their unique, irreplaceable characters.

The economic rationale is no longer reasonable if it gives rise to a barbaric ideology that says some human beings are more important than others.

The economic rationale is no longer reasonable if it forgets the objectives of a society: to ensure the health and security of its members.

By itself, the economic rationale is inhumane.

*

In "The Ghost Child," I again reflect on the question of suffering.

Decidedly, it is a question our times can no longer deal with.

Is it possible to suffer and still be happy? Nowadays, most people would say no.

Yet Mélissa, my twenty-year-old heroine, who suffers from a genetic condition, is happy. Even though she often feels faint, even though she has to take a whole cocktail of antibiotics, even though she has to do an hour of respiratory physical therapy every day, she lives, has fun, laughs, loves, admires, and learns. She can save other lives . . . And, one day, give life in her turn . . .

Happiness isn't about hiding from suffering, but about integrating it into the fabric of our existence.

*

What makes a life worth living?

That question has as many answers as there are individuals on earth.

I will never allow someone to decide for me or for others.

The slightest agreement on this point between two people raises my suspicions. Once there are three, I start seeing dictatorship.

* * *

And so the book is finished.

Reading through it, I try to locate the threads that run through it.

The dominant theme is that of a secret architecture. The couple formed by the two men in the title story depends on the official couple of Geneviève and Eddy. Dr. Heymann survives the apocalypse thanks to his complicity with an animal. The duo of Constanze and Georg Nissen is in fact a virtual trio in which Mozart occupies the central place. Alba develops maternal feelings for her nephew, not her son. Séverine and Benjamin strengthen their marriage by rejecting a child, and that child becomes, instead of a means to an end, an end in itself, and idolized as such.

I also see the theme of necessary mediation. In comparing their homosexual couple with a heterosexual one, Jean and Laurent gain a better understanding of their own path, both its achievements and its frustrations. Samuel Heymann learns to love human beings through Argos, and only avoids revenge and achieves forgiveness thanks to the look in the dog's eyes. Nissen's cataloguing and publishing of Mozart's works rescues them from oblivion, and what he loves in his new wife is the composer's former companion. Alba can only understand herself thanks to Vilma's extreme actions and Magnus's reasonable intervention. As for Séverine and Benjamin, they revisit their past when they meet Mélissa, who is an ambiguous figure to them, both a symbol of redemption, since she saves them, and one of revenge, since she makes the abortion they agreed to look like murder. Even as she pulls them from one abyss, she plunges them into another.

The final theme I detect is that of symbolic embodiment. David allows Jean and Laurent to experience a virtual fatherhood, and Jean allows Geneviève to have the success and recognition she has never known. The dogs called Argos become Dr. Heymann's wife, and Miranda's mother. Mozart gives Georg Nissen the genius he was unable to demonstrate when he wrote poetry as a young man, as well as the possibility of living in close proximity to a great creator. Vilma the kidnapper represents the dark side of Alba, whereas Jonas allows her to find fulfilment as a surrogate mother. As for young Mélissa, she embodies the child rejected by Séverine and Benjamin.

*

Bruno and Yann also point out to me that all these stories are about love.

That's so natural to me, I hadn't even noticed it. Have I ever written a story about anything else?

Foreign readers will be delighted and will again think of it as "typically French!"

*

There is something that has surprised me ever since I first started out: I only realize the coherence of my work in hindsight. Unity is not something I aim at, but something I discover. Sentences, characters, situations, and stories leak from my brain like juice.

Although it may dream of Burgundy or Bordeaux, a Beaujolais vine can only produce Beaujolais.

About the Author

Eric-Emmanuel Schmitt, playwright, novelist, and author of short stories, was awarded the French Academy's Grand Prix du Théâtre in 2001. He is one of Europe's most popular authors. His many novels and story collections include *The Most Beautiful Book in the World* (Europa Editions, 2009), *The Woman with the Bouquet* (Europa Editions, 2010), *Concerto to the Memory of an Angel* (Europa Editions, 2011) and *Three Women in a Mirror* (Europa Editions, 2013).